The Quantum Path: A Journey Beyond The Stars

Unlocking Infinite Realities Through the Power of Choice

J KUBER SINGH

To my parents,
for your endless love, support, and belief in me.

To God Shree Krishna,
for guiding me and giving me strength throughout this journey.

And to everyone who has inspired me,
this book is a reflection of your encouragement and belief in my
path.

Foreword

"The Quantum Path: A Journey Beyond The Stars" is a fictional story that follows a 17-year-old boy named Jayden, who is struggling with the pressures of school and life. Feeling overwhelmed and uncertain about his future, Jayden stumbles upon a mysterious device that introduces itself as "Q." This device offers Jayden the opportunity to explore different realities and see the outcomes of his choices.

As Jayden navigates through these alternate realities, he meets different versions of himself—some happier, some more successful, and others struggling. Each reality teaches him important lessons about the power of choice, the consequences of his actions, and the potential within him to shape his future.

Throughout the story, Jayden is guided by Q and eventually meets a mentor, Professor Alden, who helps him understand the deeper implications of his journey. With each new experience, Jayden grows more confident and begins to make better choices in his real life.

Key themes include the importance of self-awareness, the impact of small decisions, and the idea that life is shaped by the choices we make. By the end of the story, Jayden has not only learned to make more thoughtful decisions.

Preface

The journey of writing this book has been a deeply personal and transformative experience. "The Quantum Path: A Journey Beyond The Stars" began as a simple idea—a story of choices and the unknown paths that lie ahead of us. As the narrative unfolded, it became a reflection on life itself, how the decisions we make shape our futures, and the importance of understanding the impact of even the smallest actions.

In this story, I wanted to explore not only the science-fiction elements of alternate realities but also the emotional and personal growth that comes with self-discovery. The protagonist's journey mirrors the struggles we all face—the questions about who we are, where we are headed, and what it means to make meaningful choices.

This book wouldn't have been possible without the support and encouragement of those closest to me. My parents, my teachers, my editors, and the people who have inspired me along the way have all played an essential role in bringing this story to life.
 As you begin reading, I hope you find pieces of your own journey in these pages. May it inspire you to reflect on your own choices, the paths you take, and the endless possibilities that life offers.

Thank you for joining me on this adventure.

Acknowledgments

I would like to begin by expressing my deepest gratitude to **God Shree Krishna** for guiding me through every step of this journey.

To my parents **P Deepa Singh and V Jaipal Singh**, thank you for your endless support, love, and encouragement. Your belief in me has been my greatest motivation.

A special thanks to my editors, **Spandana J and Kedar B Nayak**, for your invaluable feedback and guidance in shaping this manuscript.

I also want to thank my teachers and the educational institutions that have contributed to my growth, both personally and professionally.

Lastly, to everyone who has supported me along the way.

Thank You.

Contents

Contents

Chapter 1: The Awakening

The sun was setting, painting the sky in shades of orange and pink, as 17-year-old Jayden sat in his room, staring at his open notebook. The math problems on the page looked like a foreign language, and he couldn't bring himself to care about them. His thoughts were elsewhere, tangled in worries about the future.

"What's the point of all this?" he muttered to himself. School, exams, endless homework—it all felt overwhelming, like a weight pressing down on him. What if he failed? What if he couldn't make something of himself?

Jayden pushed his notebook aside and leaned back in his chair, closing his eyes. He wished he could just escape from everything, even if just for a moment.

Just then, a soft, metallic clink interrupted his thoughts. Jayden opened his eyes and glanced down at the floor. Something small and shiny had fallen from his desk. Curious, he bent down to pick it up.

It was a strange-looking device, smooth and cool to the touch. It had no buttons, just a single screen that flickered to life as he held it. A calm, almost robotic voice spoke, making Jayden jump.

"Welcome, Jayden."

His heart raced as he looked around the room, half-expecting to see someone hiding in the shadows. But he was alone. The voice was coming from the device.

"Who... who are you?" Jayden stammered.

"I am Q," the voice responded, "your guide through the Quantum Path."

Jayden blinked, trying to make sense of what was happening. "The Quantum Path? What does that even mean?"

The device glowed brighter. "You have been chosen to explore different realities, to see the outcomes of your choices. Every decision you make has consequences, and now you have the chance to see them firsthand."

Jayden shook his head in disbelief. "This has to be some kind of joke."

But the device remained silent, waiting. Something about it felt... real. A part of him was terrified, but another part—a braver part—was curious. What if this was real? What if he could actually see the results of his choices before making them?

"Are you ready to begin?" Q's voice asked again, calm and steady.

Jayden hesitated for only a moment before nodding. "Yeah... I think I am."

As soon as the words left his mouth, the world around him began to change. The walls of his room shimmered, then dissolved into a swirl of colors. It was like being inside a kaleidoscope, with everything spinning and shifting around him.

Then, just as suddenly as it began, the swirling stopped. Jayden found himself standing in a familiar place—his school. But something was different. The colors were brighter, the air felt lighter, and there was an energy in the atmosphere that he couldn't quite describe.

"This is one version of your life," Q's voice echoed in his mind. "Here, you made different choices. Explore and see what could have been."

Jayden looked around, feeling a mix of excitement and fear. Was this really his life? What had he done differently here? He started walking, eager to find out.

As he wandered through the hallways, he noticed subtle changes—his locker was in a different spot, the posters on the walls advertised events he didn't recognize, and the students he passed seemed unfamiliar, even though they looked like people he knew.

He reached the cafeteria and stopped dead in his tracks. There, sitting at a table with a group of friends, was… himself. But this version of him looked different—more confident, more relaxed. This Jayden was laughing, clearly at ease with the people around him.

Jayden's heart pounded in his chest. "Is that… me?"

"It is," Q confirmed. "In this reality, you made different choices. Choices that led to a happier, more confident version of yourself."

Jayden watched as his alternate self joked with friends, his smile genuine and wide. A pang of jealousy and sadness tugged at his heart. He wanted that life, but how did he get there? What choices had he made differently?

"Can I talk to him?" Jayden asked, his voice barely a whisper.

"You can observe," Q replied, "but you cannot interact. This is just a glimpse, a lesson for you to learn."

Jayden felt a wave of disappointment, but he kept watching. As the lunch period ended, he followed his alternate self through the day, noticing the little things that made a big difference. This Jayden wasn't afraid to speak up in class, he participated in activities, and he seemed to have a clear direction in life.

By the time the day ended, Jayden felt a heavy weight settle in his chest. He had always thought his problems were out of his control, that he was just unlucky or not good enough. But seeing this version of himself, he realized that maybe—just maybe—he had more power over his life than he thought.

As the sun set and the world around him began to dissolve again, Q's voice broke through his thoughts. "You have seen what could be, Jayden. Remember, every choice you make shapes your future."

Jayden nodded slowly, the lesson sinking in. "I understand."

When the swirling colors faded, Jayden found himself back in his room, the device still in his hand. Everything looked the same, but he felt different—more aware, more determined.

He set the device down on his desk and picked up his notebook again. The math problems were still there, still difficult, but now he saw them differently. They weren't just numbers on a page—they were a choice, a challenge that he could either face or run from.

Jayden picked up his pen and started working on the first problem. It was hard, but he pushed through, one step at a time. Because now, he knew that every small choice mattered. And he was ready to start making better ones.

Chapter 2: The First Jump

The next morning, Jayden woke up with a strange feeling in his chest—like excitement mixed with nervousness. The device, which he had placed on his desk the night before, sat there quietly, as if waiting for him.

He got ready for school, but his thoughts kept drifting back to what had happened the previous evening. Had it all been real? It seemed impossible, but the memories were vivid. The other version of himself—the confident, happy Jayden—had felt so real.

Before heading out the door, Jayden picked up the device and slipped it into his backpack. He didn't know what might happen today, but he wasn't going to leave it behind.

School went by in a blur. Jayden found it hard to focus on his classes, his mind constantly wandering back to the possibilities the device had shown him. He wanted to know more. What other versions of his life were out there? What other choices could he explore?

When the final bell rang, Jayden didn't go straight home. Instead, he found a quiet spot in the school's library, a place where he could be alone. He pulled the device out of his backpack and held it in his hands.

"Q?" he said softly, feeling a bit foolish for talking to a gadget. But almost immediately, the screen lit up, and the now-familiar voice responded.

"I'm here, Jayden. Are you ready to explore further?"

Jayden nodded, even though no one could see him. "Yes. I want to see more. I want to understand… everything."

The device glowed brighter, and the air around Jayden seemed to hum with energy. "Then let's take the first jump."

Before Jayden could ask what that meant, the world around him blurred, and he felt a strange sensation, like he was being pulled through a tunnel of light. It was both exhilarating and terrifying.

When the light faded, Jayden found himself standing in a completely different place. He wasn't in the library anymore. Instead, he was outside, in what looked like a small, quiet town. The buildings were old but well-kept, and the streets were lined with trees.

"Where am I?" Jayden asked, turning in a circle to take in his surroundings.

"This is a different version of your life," Q explained. "In this reality, you made a decision that led you here. Explore and learn from what you see."

Jayden's heart raced as he started walking down the street. The town felt familiar, like something out of a distant memory, but he couldn't quite place it. As he walked, he noticed people waving to him, smiling warmly as if they knew him.

He passed by a small café, its windows fogged from the warmth inside. Through the glass, he saw a group of teenagers laughing and talking over coffee. One of them looked up and waved at him—a girl with bright eyes and a friendly smile. Jayden didn't recognize her, but something about her seemed… important.

"Do I know her?" Jayden asked Q.

"In this reality, she is a close friend," Q responded. "A friend you made because you chose to join the after-school art club. That decision changed many things for you."

Jayden's eyes widened. "Art club? But... I've never been into art."

"Not in your current reality," Q said. "But here, you decided to give it a try, and it led to new friendships and a different path in life."

Jayden felt a pang of curiosity. What else was different in this world? He kept walking, feeling a mix of awe and confusion as he passed familiar faces he didn't actually know.

Eventually, Jayden reached a small park at the edge of town. The sun was beginning to set, casting long shadows across the grass. There, sitting on a bench, was another version of himself—this time, slightly older, maybe by a couple of years. This Jayden was sketching in a notebook, his face calm and focused.

Jayden approached cautiously, not wanting to disturb the scene. He peered over the other Jayden's shoulder and saw a detailed drawing of the town, capturing its charm and warmth perfectly.

"He looks... happy," Jayden murmured, more to himself than to Q.

"He is," Q agreed. "In this reality, you found joy in expressing yourself through art. It gave you a sense of purpose, a way to connect with others."

Jayden watched as his alternate self continued to draw, seemingly lost in the moment. A part of him envied the peacefulness this version of him seemed to have found. In his own life, he often felt lost, unsure of what he wanted or who he was supposed to be.

"Can I... can I ever be like that?" Jayden asked quietly.

"You can," Q replied, "if you're willing to take chances, to try new things, and to make choices that align with who you truly are. Every path is different, but they all start with a single step."

Jayden nodded, absorbing the words. He realized that he had been holding back in his own life, too afraid to step out of his comfort zone. But maybe, just maybe, it was time to change that.

As the sun dipped lower in the sky, the world around him began to shimmer again. Jayden knew what was coming, but this time, he felt ready. When the colors swirled and the park faded away, he wasn't scared. Instead, he felt a sense of resolve building inside him.

When he returned to his own world, sitting once again in the school library, Jayden took a deep breath. The device in his hand had gone quiet, its screen dark, but the lessons he had learned were still buzzing in his mind.

He packed up his things and left the library, feeling a bit different than before. As he walked home, he found himself thinking about what new things he might try—things that could lead him down a path he hadn't even considered before.

The first jump had shown him that his life wasn't set in stone. It was full of possibilities, waiting for him to explore. And now, Jayden was ready to start making those choices.

Chapter 3: Meeting the Mentor

Jayden couldn't shake the feeling of excitement and curiosity that had taken hold of him since his first two experiences with the Quantum Path. The possibilities seemed endless, and for the first time in a long while, he felt like he was in control of his own destiny. He was eager to learn more, to dive deeper into the choices he hadn't yet made.

But what he wasn't expecting was that the next part of his journey would involve meeting someone who would change the way he saw everything.

The following day at school was unusually normal. Jayden attended his classes, did his work, and exchanged small talk with his friends. Yet, his mind was elsewhere, replaying the images of the different lives he had glimpsed. When the last bell rang, he felt the now-familiar pull to explore the Quantum Path again.

Instead of heading straight home, Jayden wandered to a quiet park near his house. It was a peaceful spot, with tall trees and a small pond where ducks often paddled lazily. Finding a secluded bench, he pulled out the device. He didn't need to speak this time; as soon as he touched it, the screen lit up, and Q's voice filled the air.

"Ready to continue, Jayden?"

"Yeah," Jayden replied, his voice steady. "But... what's next? I've seen different versions of my life, but I don't know what I'm supposed to do with all this."

"Learning about your choices is only the beginning," Q said. "To truly understand the Quantum Path, you need guidance—someone who can help you make sense of the possibilities and the responsibilities that come with them."

Jayden frowned. "Guidance? You mean like a teacher?"

"Yes, a mentor," Q confirmed. "Someone who has walked this path before and can help you navigate your journey."

Before Jayden could ask more, the world around him began to shimmer and blur, just as it had before. The colors swirled, and he felt himself being pulled through that strange tunnel of light.

When the sensation finally stopped, he found himself standing in a place that was both familiar and unfamiliar.

He was in a large, airy room filled with books—hundreds, maybe thousands of them—lining shelves that reached up to a high, domed ceiling. The room smelled of old paper and a hint of something sweet, like cinnamon. In the center of the room stood a tall, older man with silver hair and kind eyes. He looked up from a book he was reading and smiled warmly at Jayden.

"Welcome, Jayden," the man said, closing the book and setting it aside. "I've been expecting you."

Jayden blinked in surprise. "You... you know me?"

The man chuckled softly. "In a way, yes. My name is Professor Alden, and I'm here to help you understand the choices that lie before you."

Jayden felt a mix of relief and apprehension. This man, Professor Alden, seemed wise and calm, like someone who had seen much more of the world than Jayden could imagine. But he also felt a bit nervous, unsure of what to say or do next.

"How... how do you know about the Quantum Path?" Jayden asked hesitantly.

Professor Alden gestured for Jayden to sit in a comfortable chair by the fireplace, where the flames crackled softly. "I was once like you," he began, settling into his own chair across from Jayden. "Curious, uncertain, and eager to explore the many paths that life has to offer. The
Quantum Path found me when I was around your age, and it changed my life forever."

Jayden leaned forward, intrigued. "So, you've seen other versions of your life too?"

"Indeed," Alden nodded. "I've walked many paths, seen many possibilities. Some were filled with joy and success, others with challenges and heartache. But each path taught me something valuable. And now, I use what I've learned to help others like you."

Jayden felt a spark of hope. "So you're here to help me figure out what to do? How to make the right choices?"

"Not exactly," Alden said gently. "I can't tell you what choices to make— that's something only you can decide. But I can help you see the bigger picture, to understand that every choice you make, big or small, has consequences. Some you'll see right away, others may take years to reveal themselves."

Jayden nodded slowly, trying to absorb what Professor Alden was saying. "But how do I know what the right choice is? What if I mess up?"

Alden smiled kindly. "There's no such thing as a perfect choice, Jayden. Life is about learning, growing, and sometimes making mistakes. The important thing is to keep moving forward, to keep exploring and asking questions. The Quantum Path will show you the possibilities, but it's up to you to choose the path that feels right for you."

Jayden thought about this, feeling both comforted and a bit overwhelmed. "So... where do I start?"

Alden's eyes twinkled with a knowing look. "Start by being open to new experiences. Don't be afraid to try something different, even if it seems small or insignificant. You never know what doors it might open."

Jayden felt a warmth in his chest, like a small flame of courage had been lit. "I think I understand," he said quietly.

Professor Alden reached over and placed a gentle hand on Jayden's shoulder. "Remember, Jayden, the path you choose today will shape the person you become tomorrow. Trust yourself, and don't be afraid to take that first step."

As Jayden absorbed these words, the room around him began to blur and fade, just like before. But this time, he felt a sense of peace, like he had gained something important, something that would stay with him.

When he opened his eyes again, he was back in the park, the device still in his hand. The sun was beginning to set, casting a warm glow over the trees. Jayden took a deep breath, feeling more grounded than he had in a long time.

He stood up, ready to head home, but this time with a clearer mind and a stronger resolve. Professor Alden's words echoed in his mind: "The path you choose today will shape the person you become tomorrow."

Jayden smiled to himself. He was ready to start making choices that mattered, choices that would lead him down the path he wanted to walk.

Chapter 4: The Fork in the Road

The next few days were unlike any Jayden had ever experienced. Armed with the wisdom from Professor Alden and the mysterious device in his possession, he began to see his world differently. Choices were no longer random acts; they were deliberate steps on a path that only he could choose. Every moment seemed to carry a new significance, and for the first time, Jayden felt a sense of control over his future.

But life, as Jayden was about to learn, often throws unexpected challenges when you least expect them.

It was a Friday afternoon, and the school was buzzing with excitement. The weekend was just around the corner, and everyone seemed eager to unwind. Jayden, however, had something else on his mind. The device had been quiet since his last encounter with Professor Alden, but he felt a strange sense of anticipation, like something big was about to happen.

As he walked through the crowded hallway, Jayden spotted his friend Marcus, who was leaning against his locker with a worried expression on his face. Marcus was usually the life of the party, always cracking jokes and keeping everyone entertained. But today, he looked different—tense, even.

"Hey, Marcus, you okay?" Jayden asked as he approached.

Marcus glanced up, forcing a smile that didn't quite reach his eyes. "Oh, hey, Jayden. Yeah,

I'm fine. Just... got some stuff on my mind."

Jayden could tell something was bothering him. "You sure? You don't look fine."

Marcus sighed, looking around to make sure no one was listening. "It's just... I'm supposed to go to this big party tonight. Everyone's going to be there, and it's supposed to be crazy fun. But my grades have been slipping, and my parents said if I don't improve, they're going to ground me for the rest of the year."

Jayden frowned, understanding Marcus's dilemma. The party was a big deal—everyone had been talking about it all week—but so was school. Marcus wasn't the best student, and if his grades dropped any further, he'd be in serious trouble.

"That's a tough spot," Jayden said thoughtfully. "What are you going to do?"

Marcus shrugged, looking conflicted. "I don't know, man. If I go to the party, I'm risking everything. But if I stay home to study, I'll miss out on one of the biggest nights of the year.
What would you do?"

Jayden hesitated. A few weeks ago, he would have said to go to the party without thinking twice. But now, after everything he'd learned, he saw the situation differently. This wasn't just about one night; it was about the kind of choices that could shape their futures.

Before he could respond, the device in his pocket warmed up, and Jayden felt a familiar sensation—a subtle vibration that told him another jump was coming. He took a deep breath, knowing what he had to do.

"Marcus," Jayden said, trying to keep his voice steady, "I think you need to look at the bigger picture here. Missing one party won't be the end of the world, but tanking your grades could have a big impact on your future."

Marcus frowned, clearly not happy with the advice. "Yeah, I know. But it's just... I don't want to miss out, you know? Everyone's going to be there."

Jayden nodded, understanding the pressure. "I get it. But maybe you should think about what really matters to you. Is it worth risking your future for one night of fun?"

Marcus didn't respond immediately, his eyes distant as he thought over Jayden's words. After a moment, he sighed and nodded slowly. "Yeah, you're probably right. I'll think about it."

As Marcus walked away, Jayden felt the world around him begin to shift. The colors blurred, and once again, he was pulled through the Quantum Path. This time, however, the jump felt different—more intense, like it carried greater weight.

When the world solidified around him, Jayden found himself standing in front of a large, unfamiliar building. The sign above the entrance read "Marcus's Auto Repair." The place looked busy, with cars lined up for service and a steady flow of customers coming and going.

Jayden's heart raced as he walked closer. Inside, he could see Marcus— an older version of him—talking to a customer. This Marcus looked confident, happy even, as he explained something about the car's engine. There was a sense of pride in the way he carried himself, as though he had found his calling.

"Is this Marcus's future?" Jayden asked, not sure if Q would answer.

"One of them," Q's voice responded, echoing in his mind. "In this reality, Marcus chose to focus on his studies, worked hard, and eventually opened his own successful business. He made sacrifices, but they paid off in the long run."

Jayden watched as Marcus shook hands with the customer, smiling as they chatted. It was clear that this version of Marcus had found a path that suited him, one that brought him success and satisfaction.

But then, the scene shifted. Jayden blinked, and suddenly he was standing in a dimly lit bar. The atmosphere was completely different—loud music, laughter, and the smell of alcohol in the air. At a corner table, surrounded by empty bottles and slumped in a chair, was another version of Marcus. This Marcus looked tired, worn down by life. He was talking to someone, but his words were slurred, his eyes dull.

Jayden's heart sank. "What happened here?"

"In this reality," Q explained, "Marcus chose the easy path—partying, avoiding responsibility, and neglecting his studies. His life became a series of short-term pleasures, but he never found true fulfillment. The choices he made led him down a path of regret."

Jayden felt a chill run down his spine. The difference between the two versions of Marcus was stark—one had built a life of success, the other had fallen into a cycle of emptiness. And it all started with a single choice.

The world began to blur again, but this time, Jayden wasn't scared. He knew what he had to do.

When he returned to the hallway at school, Marcus was still standing by his locker, looking conflicted. Jayden approached him, feeling a surge of determination.

"Marcus," Jayden said firmly, "I know it's hard, but I really think you should stay home and study tonight. The party will be fun, sure, but your future is more important. You don't want to look back and regret this decision."

Marcus looked at him, surprised by the intensity in Jayden's voice. He hesitated for a moment, then nodded slowly. "Yeah... yeah, you're right. I'll hit the books tonight."

Jayden smiled, relieved. "Good choice, Marcus. You won't regret it."

As Jayden walked away, he felt a sense of accomplishment. For the first time, he had used what he had learned from the Quantum Path to help someone else. It wasn't just about his choices anymore—it was about making a difference in the lives of those around him.

And as he left the school, the device in his pocket warmed again, a subtle reminder that this was only the beginning.

Chapter 5: The Ripple Effect

Jayden had started to realize that the choices he made—and even the advice he gave—could have a profound impact on the lives of those around him. The experience with Marcus had opened his eyes to the interconnectedness of their lives, and it made him wonder: How many other lives could be affected by a single decision?

It was Saturday morning, and Jayden found himself sitting at the kitchen table, staring out the window. The neighbourhood was peaceful, with the sound of birds chirping and the occasional bark of a dog in the distance. But Jayden's mind was racing, replaying the events of the past few days.

The device sat quietly beside him, its screen dark. Jayden had noticed that it only seemed to activate when something important was about to happen, as if it could sense the gravity of the moment. He wondered if today would bring another jump, another lesson.

"Jayden, are you okay?" His mom's voice broke through his thoughts. She was standing by the counter, holding a cup of coffee, her eyes filled with concern.

"Yeah, I'm fine, Mom," Jayden replied, forcing a smile. "Just thinking about stuff."

His mom smiled back, but there was a hint of worry in her expression. "You've been a little quiet lately. If there's something on your mind, you know you can talk to me, right?"

Jayden hesitated. He wanted to tell her about the device, about the Quantum Path and everything he had experienced, but he wasn't sure how to explain it without sounding crazy.
Instead, he nodded and said, "I know, Mom. Thanks."

She studied him for a moment, then seemed to decide to let it go. "Okay, just remember, I'm here if you need me."

Jayden appreciated her concern, but he knew this was something he had to figure out on his own. After finishing breakfast, he decided to go for a walk to clear his head. The device, as always, went into his pocket.

As he walked through the neighbourhood, Jayden's thoughts kept circling back to Marcus. Had he really made the right decision? What if Marcus resented him for convincing him to skip the party? What if it led to something worse?

Lost in thought, Jayden didn't notice the group of kids playing in the park until he nearly bumped into them. A soccer ball rolled to his feet, and a little boy, no older than seven or eight, ran up to retrieve it.

"Sorry, mister!" the boy said, flashing a gap-toothed grin as he grabbed the ball.

Jayden smiled back. "No problem, kiddo. Have fun!"

The boy ran back to his friends, and Jayden continued walking, but his mind was now on something else: the impact of small actions. He had barely noticed the kids, but they were living their lives, making their own choices, just like he was. How many times had he made a decision that, without realizing it, affected someone else?

As if in response to his thoughts, the device in his pocket vibrated gently. Jayden stopped walking and pulled it out. The screen lit up, and Q's voice came through, soft but clear.

"Jayden, are you ready to see the ripple effect of your choices?"

Jayden's heart skipped a beat. "Ripple effect? You mean... how one choice can affect a lot of things?"

"Exactly," Q replied. "Every action, no matter how small, creates ripples that spread far and wide. Sometimes, those ripples return to us in ways we don't expect."

Before Jayden could ask more, the world around him began to shift once again. The familiar sensation of being pulled through the Quantum Path took over, and Jayden braced himself for whatever was coming next.

When the world solidified, Jayden found himself standing in front of a large building that looked like a school, but not one he recognized. It was modern, with large windows and a wide lawn out front. Kids of all ages were playing, laughing, and chatting as they moved toward the entrance.

"Where am I?" Jayden asked, looking around.

"This is a future possibility," Q explained. "In this reality, you chose to pursue a career in education, inspired by the advice you gave to Marcus. You saw how your words could influence others, and you wanted to make a difference on a larger scale."

Jayden blinked, surprised. "Me? A teacher?"

"Yes," Q said. "You realized that helping others find their path was something you were passionate about. So you studied, worked hard, and eventually became a teacher, guiding students toward their own futures."

As Jayden processed this, he saw a group of students running toward him, calling his name. They looked up to him with respect and admiration, and he could see in their eyes that they valued his guidance.

"Mr. Kuber!" one of the students called out, waving enthusiastically. "Are you coming to the game tonight?"

Jayden smiled at the kid, feeling a strange warmth in his chest. "Wouldn't miss it for the world," he heard himself say.

The scene shifted again, and this time Jayden found himself in a different setting—a small office, cluttered with papers and books. He was sitting behind a desk, talking to a young woman who looked to be in her late teens. She was visibly upset, tears streaming down her face as she spoke.

"I just don't know what to do," she said, her voice trembling. "Everything feels so overwhelming. I don't know if I can make it."

Jayden felt a deep empathy for the girl, as if he had known her for years. "It's okay to feel that way," he heard himself say gently. "But you're stronger than you think. Remember, every choice you make is a step forward, even if it's a small one. You don't have to have it all figured out right now."

The girl nodded, wiping her eyes, and Jayden could see a glimmer of hope returning to her expression. "Thank you," she whispered. "I... I think I can do this."

Jayden felt a surge of pride and compassion. In this reality, he had become someone who helped others navigate their own Quantum Paths, someone who made a tangible difference in the lives of others.

But then the scene shifted once more, and Jayden found himself back in the park. This time, it was quiet, almost eerily so. The kids who had been playing earlier were gone, and the sun was setting, casting long shadows across the grass.

Jayden noticed a figure sitting on a bench nearby. It was an older version of himself, but this Jayden looked tired, worn down by life. His hair was graying, and there was a deep sadness in his eyes. He sat alone, staring at the ground, as if lost in thoughts of what might have been.

"Who is this?" Jayden asked quietly, dreading the answer.

"This is another possible future," Q said softly. "In this reality, you chose to ignore the importance of your actions. You made choices without thinking about their impact on others, and over time, those decisions led you to a life of regret and isolation."

Jayden felt a lump in his throat as he watched the older version of himself, sitting alone in the fading light. It was a stark contrast to the life he had seen just moments ago—a life filled with purpose and connection.

The world began to blur again, and Jayden was pulled back to his own reality. When he opened his eyes, he was standing in the park, the device still warm in his hand. The sun was beginning to set, just like in the vision.

Jayden took a deep breath, feeling a mix of emotions. He knew now that every choice he made was like a stone thrown into a pond, creating ripples that spread far beyond what he could see. Those ripples could lead to a life of fulfillment and connection, or they could lead to regret and loneliness.

As he walked back home, Jayden made a silent promise to himself: He would think carefully about the choices he made, not just for his own sake, but for the sake of those around him. He wanted to create positive ripples, to make a difference in the world, no matter how small.

And with that thought, Jayden felt a renewed sense of purpose, knowing that the path ahead was his to shape.

Chapter 6: A Leap of Faith

The following week felt different for Jayden. With every passing day, he became more aware of how the small, everyday choices he made could shape not just his future but the futures of those around him. The experience with the Quantum Path had changed him in ways he hadn't fully anticipated.

It was a crisp Tuesday morning when Jayden arrived at school, his backpack slung over one shoulder. The hallways were buzzing with the usual chatter—students discussing last night's homework, the upcoming football game, and weekend plans. But Jayden's thoughts were elsewhere, still focused on the lesson from the Quantum Path.

As he made his way to his locker, he saw Zoey and Emma deep in conversation. Zoey, with her fiery red hair and sharp wit, was laughing at something Emma had said. Emma, on the other hand, was quieter, more introspective, with a soft smile that rarely left her face.

Jayden hesitated for a moment, watching them. The last time he had talked to Zoey, she had seemed stressed about something, but he hadn't asked her about it. Now, with everything he had learned, he wondered if maybe he should have.

"Hey, Jayden!" Zoey called out when she spotted him. "You okay? You look like you're in deep thought or something."

Jayden forced a grin, trying to push aside the heaviness in his chest. "Yeah, just... thinking about life, you know?"

Zoey raised an eyebrow. "Life, huh? Sounds deep. Anything you want to share?"

Jayden shrugged, unsure how to put his thoughts into words. "Just... I've been thinking a lot about how the choices we make can affect everything. Not just for us, but for everyone around us too."

Emma nodded thoughtfully. "That's true. It's like that butterfly effect thing, right? One small action can lead to big changes down the line."

Jayden was about to respond when he noticed something. Zoey's smile didn't quite reach her eyes, and there was a tension in her posture that made him pause.

"Zoey, are you okay?" Jayden asked, his voice gentle.

Zoey's expression faltered for a moment before she quickly recovered. "Yeah, I'm fine. Why do you ask?"

Jayden hesitated, feeling that familiar nudge from the Quantum Path. "I just... you seem a little off today. If something's bothering you, you can talk to us, you know."

Zoey looked at him, her guard up for just a second, then sighed. "It's nothing, really. Just some family stuff. My parents have been fighting a lot lately, and it's been stressing me out."

Emma placed a comforting hand on Zoey's arm. "I'm sorry to hear that, Zoey. That sounds really tough."

Jayden nodded, feeling a surge of empathy for his friend. "If you ever need to talk, we're here for you."

Zoey smiled weakly. "Thanks, guys. I appreciate it."

The bell rang, signaling the start of the first period, and they all began to head to their classes. But as Jayden walked to his classroom, he couldn't shake the feeling that there was more he could do. The lessons from the

Quantum Path had shown him that sometimes, even the smallest actions could have a big impact. Maybe he couldn't solve Zoey's problems, but he could at least be there for her.

The day passed in a blur of lectures, assignments, and the usual routine. Jayden tried to focus on his classes, but his mind kept drifting back to Zoey. He couldn't help but wonder how her family situation was affecting her, and what he could do to help.

As the final bell rang and students began to file out of the building, Jayden made a decision. He caught up with Zoey as she was heading to her locker.

"Hey, Zoey," Jayden called out, jogging to catch up with her. "Do you want to hang out after school today? Maybe grab some ice cream or something?"

Zoey looked at him, surprised by the sudden invitation. "Uh, sure, I guess. I could use a distraction."

Jayden smiled, feeling a sense of relief. "Great! There's this new place that just opened up downtown. I heard they have the best sundaes."

Zoey nodded, a small smile tugging at her lips. "Sounds good. Thanks, Jayden."

They walked out of the school together, the cool afternoon breeze ruffling their hair. As they made their way to the ice cream shop, Jayden noticed that Zoey seemed to relax a little, her usual spark slowly returning.

When they arrived, the shop was bustling with activity. The smell of freshly made waffles and the sound of laughter filled the air. They found a small table by the window and ordered their sundaes.

As they waited for their ice cream, Jayden decided to take a leap of faith. "Zoey, I know you said it's just family stuff, but if you want to talk about it, I'm here to listen."

Zoey was silent for a moment, staring out the window. Then she sighed and turned back to him. "It's just… my parents have been fighting a lot lately. They're talking about separating, and I'm scared of what that means for our family."

Jayden's heart went out to her. "I'm really sorry, Zoey. That must be so hard to deal with."

Zoey nodded, her eyes glassy. "It is. I just… I don't know what to do. I feel so helpless."

Jayden reached across the table and took her hand, offering a comforting squeeze. "You're not alone in this. You've got me, and Emma, and all your other friends. We're here for you, no matter what happens."

Zoey looked at him, her eyes softening. "Thanks, Jayden. That means a lot."

Their sundaes arrived, and for a while, they just enjoyed the simple pleasure of ice cream and good company. The tension in Zoey's shoulders seemed to ease as they laughed and joked about random things. By the time they finished, she seemed more like her old self.

As they walked back home, Zoey turned to Jayden and said, "You know, I was really down this morning, but spending time with you helped a lot. I'm glad you asked me to hang out."

Jayden smiled, feeling a warm glow in his chest. "I'm glad too. Sometimes, we just need a break from everything."

They parted ways at the corner of Zoey's street, and as Jayden watched her walk home, he felt a deep sense of satisfaction. He hadn't solved Zoey's problems, but he had been there for her when she needed it most. And that, he realized, was just as important.

As he walked the rest of the way home, the device in his pocket vibrated gently, as if acknowledging his efforts. Jayden pulled it out and saw a message flash on the screen:

"Every leap of faith creates ripples of change. Keep going."

Jayden smiled, tucking the device back into his pocket. He didn't know what the future held, but he was ready to face it, one choice at a time.

Chapter 7: The Road Less Travelled

Jayden woke up the next morning with a sense of clarity that he hadn't felt in a long time. The experiences of the past few weeks had changed him in ways he was only beginning to understand. Each step along the Quantum Path had opened his eyes to the power of his choices, and now, he felt ready to take on whatever came next.

As he got ready for school, Jayden found himself reflecting on his future. For the first time, he felt like he had a real say in what that future might look like. He didn't know exactly where his path would lead, but he knew that he wanted to make decisions that aligned with his values—decisions that would create positive ripples in the world around him.

During breakfast, Jayden's mom noticed the change in his demeanour. "You seem more upbeat today," she commented with a smile as she sipped her coffee.

Jayden grinned back. "Yeah, I guess I just feel more… focused. Like I have a better idea of what I want to do."

His mom raised an eyebrow, intrigued. "Oh? Care to share?"

Jayden hesitated for a moment, then decided to go for it. "I've been thinking a lot about my future—what I want to do after high school. I know it's still a while away, but I want to start making choices that will help me get where I want to go."

His mom smiled warmly, pride evident in her eyes. "That's great, Jayden. It's never too early to start planning for the future. Do you have any ideas in mind?"

Jayden nodded slowly, gathering his thoughts. "I'm not sure yet, but I think I want to do something that helps people. Maybe teaching, or counselling, or something like that. I want to make a difference, you know?"

His mom reached across the table and squeezed his hand. "I'm so proud of you, Jayden.

Whatever path you choose, I know you'll do great things."

Jayden felt a surge of warmth at her words. "Thanks, Mom. That means a lot."

The day at school passed quickly, with Jayden more focused than ever. He paid closer attention in his classes, took notes with a renewed sense of purpose, and even found himself volunteering to help a classmate who was struggling with math. It was a small gesture, but it felt good to lend a hand.

At lunch, Jayden sat with Zoey, Emma, and Marcus. The group had become closer since the Quantum Path had first appeared in Jayden's life, and he appreciated their support more than ever.

"So, Jayden," Marcus began, leaning forward with a mischievous grin, "what's next on your grand plan to save the world?"

Jayden chuckled, shaking his head. "I'm not trying to save the world, Marcus. Just trying to figure out my place in it."

Emma nodded thoughtfully. "That's a pretty big deal, though. I think we all want to make a difference in our own way."

Zoey, who had been quiet up until now, chimed in. "Jayden's right, though. The choices we make now will shape our futures. It's kind of exciting to think about, but also a little scary."

Jayden smiled at his friends, feeling grateful for their support. "Yeah, it is. But I think as long as we stick together and keep each other grounded, we'll figure it out."

As the conversation continued, Jayden felt a sense of camaraderie with his friends that he hadn't experienced before. They were all in this together, navigating the complexities of life and the choices that came with it.

After school, Jayden decided to take a different route home. It was a longer path that wound through a quiet neighbourhood, lined with tall trees and well-kept gardens. As he walked, he thought about how the Quantum Path had shown him different possibilities for his future. Each choice he made would lead him down a different road, and while some of those roads were uncertain, they all had the potential to lead to something meaningful.

As he turned a corner, Jayden noticed an older man sitting on a bench in a small park, reading a book. The man looked up as Jayden approached and gave him a friendly nod.

"Afternoon," the man said with a smile. "Taking the scenic route home?"

Jayden smiled back. "Yeah, just felt like a change of pace."

The man closed his book, setting it down beside him. "Sometimes it's good to take a different path. You never know what you might discover along the way."

Jayden paused, considering the man's words. "That's true. I've been thinking about that a lot lately."

The man raised an eyebrow, intrigued. "Oh? What's on your mind?"

Jayden wasn't sure why, but he felt comfortable talking to this stranger. There was something about him that put Jayden at ease. "I've just been thinking about the future, and how the choices I make now could affect where I end up."

The man nodded, a knowing look in his eyes. "Ah, the crossroads of life. It's a place we all find ourselves at some point. The important thing is to trust your instincts and stay true to yourself."

Jayden smiled, appreciating the man's wisdom. "That's what I'm trying to do. It's not always easy, though."

The man chuckled softly. "No, it's not. But the road less travelled often leads to the most rewarding destinations. Just remember, the journey is just as important as the destination."

Jayden felt a sense of calm wash over him as he listened to the man's words. "Thanks. I think I needed to hear that."

The man nodded, picking up his book again. "Anytime, young man. Take care of yourself."

As Jayden continued his walk home, he felt lighter, as if a weight had been lifted from his shoulders. The conversation with the man had reinforced what he already knew deep down: that the choices he made were his own, and that by staying true to himself, he could navigate whatever life threw his way.

When he got home, Jayden went straight to his room, pulled out his journal, and began to write. He wrote about the Quantum Path, the lessons he had learned, and the people who had helped him along the way. He wrote about his hopes for the future and the choices he wanted to make.

And as he wrote, the device in his pocket remained silent, content to let Jayden take the lead.

Chapter 8: The Power of Perspective

The next few days passed in a blur, with Jayden focusing on schoolwork, spending time with his friends, and continuing to reflect on the choices he was making. The lessons from the Quantum Path had taken root in his mind, and he found himself approaching everyday situations with a new sense of awareness.

One evening, as Jayden was finishing up his homework, he received a text from Emma.

Emma: *Hey, are you free tomorrow after school? I need to talk to you about something.*

Jayden's curiosity was piqued. It wasn't like Emma to be vague, and her message had a sense of urgency to it.

Jayden: *Sure, what's up? Everything okay?*

There was a pause before Emma replied.

Emma: *Yeah, everything's fine. I just need your perspective on something. Can we meet at the park after school?*

Jayden agreed, and the next day, he found himself heading to the park, wondering what Emma wanted to talk about. When he arrived, he saw her sitting on a bench under a large oak tree, her expression thoughtful.

"Hey, Emma," Jayden greeted her as he approached. "What's on your mind?"

Emma looked up at him, a small smile on her face. "Hey, Jayden. Thanks for meeting me. I just… I needed to talk to someone I trust."

Jayden sat down beside her, sensing that whatever was on her mind was important. "Of course. What's going on?"

Emma took a deep breath before she began. "I've been feeling really conflicted lately. You know how we're all supposed to start thinking about our future plans, right? Like college, careers, all that stuff?"

Jayden nodded. "Yeah, it's been on my mind a lot too."

Emma sighed, her gaze drifting to the ground. "The thing is, I've always thought I wanted to go to college, get a good job, and do the whole 'successful life' thing. But lately, I've been questioning if that's really what I want. I'm not sure if it's my dream or just what everyone expects me to do."

Jayden listened intently, understanding her dilemma. "That's a tough situation. It's hard to know if you're following your own path or just doing what others expect."

Emma nodded; her expression pensive. "Exactly. And I feel like I'm at a crossroads. On one hand, I want to follow my passion for art, even though it's not the most 'practical' choice. On the other hand, I know that the safe route would be to go to college, get a stable job, and have a secure future. But… I don't want to live with regrets, you know?"

Jayden could see the conflict in her eyes, and he understood the weight of the decision she was facing. "I get it, Emma. It's hard to choose between what you're passionate about and what feels safe. But I think the important thing is to be honest with yourself about what you really want."

Emma looked at him, her expression softening. "That's what I've been struggling with. I keep thinking about what my parents want for me, what society expects, and what my friends are doing. But when I think about what I want, I get scared. What if I make the wrong choice?"

Jayden thought back to the lessons he had learned from the Quantum Path. "I don't think there's a 'wrong' choice, Emma. Every path has its own challenges and rewards. The important thing is to choose the path that feels right for you, even if it's not the easiest or most popular choice."

Emma was silent for a moment, letting his words sink in. "That's easier said than done. But you're right. I guess I just need to trust myself more."

Jayden nodded, giving her a reassuring smile. "You're stronger and more capable than you think, Emma. And whatever path you choose, you'll find a way to make it work. Just remember that you're not alone. We're all figuring this out together."

Emma's expression softened, and she reached out to squeeze Jayden's hand. "Thanks, Jayden.

I really needed to hear that. It's nice to have someone who understands."

Jayden squeezed her hand back, feeling a deep sense of connection with his friend. "Anytime,

Emma. I'm always here for you."

They sat in comfortable silence for a while, watching the sun begin to set behind the trees. The sky was painted in shades of orange and pink, and the air was cool and refreshing. It was one of those moments where everything felt peaceful and right with the world.

As they sat there, Jayden found himself reflecting on his own journey. The Quantum Path had shown him the importance of perspective—of looking at life from different angles and understanding that there were many ways to approach any situation. It had taught him that the choices he made didn't have to be perfect; they just had to be true to who he was.

After a while, Emma turned to him, her expression more relaxed. "You know, I think I'm going to take a chance on my art. It's what I'm passionate about, and I don't want to live with regrets. I'll still keep my options open, but I think it's time I start trusting myself more."

Jayden smiled, feeling proud of her decision. "I think that's a great choice, Emma. You have an amazing talent, and the world needs more people who follow their passions."

Emma grinned, the weight on her shoulders seeming to lift. "Thanks, Jayden. You've helped me more than you know."

As they stood up to leave, Jayden felt a sense of fulfilment. He had helped Emma gain clarity, and in doing so, he had also solidified his own understanding of the lessons he had learned. The Quantum Path wasn't just about making the right choices; it was about seeing the bigger picture, understanding the impact of those choices, and helping others find their own way.

As they walked home together, Jayden felt the device in his pocket vibrate once again. He pulled it out and saw a new message flash across the screen:

"Perspective is the key to understanding. Keep sharing your light with others."

Jayden smiled, tucking the device back into his pocket. He knew that the journey was far from over, but with each step, he was becoming more confident in his ability to navigate the path ahead.

And with friends like Emma by his side, he knew that he wasn't walking that path alone.

Chapter 9: The Ripple Effect

Jayden's days had settled into a new rhythm—one where each decision he made felt more intentional, more aligned with who he wanted to be. The experiences with the Quantum Path had changed him, and he found himself increasingly aware of how his actions impacted the world around him.

One afternoon, during a quiet moment in the library, Jayden was flipping through a book for an assignment when he overheard a conversation at a nearby table. A group of younger students were talking in hushed voices, clearly upset about something.

"I just don't get it," one of them said, frustration evident in his tone. "No matter how hard I try, I can't seem to keep up in class. I'm always behind."

Jayden glanced over, recognizing the boy as one of the quieter students from his math class.

The boy's friends tried to console him, but Jayden could see that their words weren't enough to lift his spirits.

After a moment of hesitation, Jayden decided to approach them. "Hey, I couldn't help but overhear. Are you guys talking about math class?"

The younger students looked up in surprise. The boy who had been speaking looked a bit embarrassed, but he nodded. "Yeah. I'm just having a hard time with it. It's like no matter what I do, I can't get the hang of it."

Jayden smiled reassuringly. "I totally get that. Math can be tough, but it's not impossible. If you want, I can help you out. I've been through the same stuff you're working on now."

The boy's eyes widened in surprise. "Really? You'd do that?"

"Of course," Jayden replied. "Sometimes all it takes is someone to explain it in a different way. We can work through it together."

The boy smiled, a little hope creeping into his expression. "Thanks, that would be awesome."

They arranged to meet after school in the library, and as Jayden walked back to his seat, he felt a sense of satisfaction. It was a small gesture, but he knew it could make a big difference.

Helping others had become an important part of his journey, and he was beginning to understand just how much of an impact one person could have.

Later that day, Jayden met with the boy, whose name he learned was Liam. They spread out their books across a table in the library, and Jayden started explaining the math problems in a way that was easier to understand. He used simple examples, breaking down the steps and making sure Liam followed along.

As they worked, Jayden noticed how Liam's confidence started to grow. With each problem they solved, Liam's frustration began to fade, replaced by a sense of accomplishment.

"You're really good at this," Liam said, looking up at Jayden with newfound respect. "I think I'm starting to get it."

Jayden smiled. "You're doing great, Liam. Sometimes it just takes a little practice and the right mindset. Keep at it, and you'll see how much easier it gets."

They continued working for another hour, and by the time they finished, Liam was smiling widely. "Thanks, Jayden. I don't feel so lost anymore. I actually feel like I can do this."

Jayden felt a warmth in his chest, knowing that he had made a difference in Liam's day. "You're welcome. Just remember, it's okay to ask for help when you need it. We're all in this together."

As they packed up their things, Liam hesitated for a moment, then spoke again. "Jayden, why did you help me? I mean, you didn't have to. Most people just ignore stuff like this."

Jayden paused, considering the question. "I guess I helped because I know what it's like to struggle with something and feel like you're on your own. And I've learned that even small actions can have a big impact. Sometimes, all it takes is one person to make a difference."

Liam nodded, looking thoughtful. "I want to do that too. Help people, I mean. It feels good."

Jayden smiled. "That's the ripple effect. When you help someone, you're creating ripples that can spread out and touch others. And who knows? Maybe one day, you'll be the one helping someone else out."

As Jayden left the library, he felt a deep sense of fulfillment. The Quantum Path had taught him that every action, no matter how small, could create ripples that spread far beyond what he could see. Helping Liam had not only brightened the boy's day, but it had also reinforced Jayden's belief in the power of kindness and support.

That evening, Jayden sat in his room, reflecting on the day's events. He had always thought of himself as just another kid trying to figure things out, but now he realized that he had the ability to influence others in a positive way. The choices he made, the way he treated people— these things mattered more than he had ever realized.

As he lay down to sleep, the device in his pocket vibrated softly. Jayden pulled it out, curious to see what message it had for him this time.

"Your actions are the stones that create ripples in the pond of life. Keep casting them wisely."

Jayden smiled as he placed the device on his nightstand. The words resonated with him deeply. The ripple effect was real, and he was determined to continue casting his stones wisely, creating positive ripples wherever he could.

As he drifted off to sleep, Jayden felt a sense of peace. The journey ahead was still full of uncertainties, but he knew that as long as he kept making choices that aligned with his values, he would continue to make a difference—in his life and in the lives of those around him.

Chapter 10: The Ultimate Test

Jayden's life had been relatively calm since he started embracing the lessons of the Quantum Path. He had grown closer to his friends, helped others, and gained a deeper understanding of himself. But as with any journey, a true test was inevitable, and Jayden was about to face his biggest challenge yet.

It all started on a seemingly ordinary day. Jayden was in the middle of a science class when the school's intercom crackled to life. "Jayden, please report to the principal's office," the voice announced. The other students exchanged curious glances as Jayden packed up his things and left the classroom, wondering what this was about.

As Jayden walked to the principal's office, he couldn't shake the feeling that something was wrong. When he arrived, he found the principal, Mr. Davies, waiting for him with a serious expression.

"Please, have a seat, Jayden," Mr. Davies said, gesturing to a chair. Jayden sat down, feeling a knot form in his stomach.

"Is something wrong?" Jayden asked, trying to keep his voice steady.

Mr. Davies sighed, folding his hands on the desk in front of him. "Jayden, there's been an incident. It involves one of your friends—Liam."

Jayden's heart sank. "What happened?"

"Liam was caught in a fight earlier today," Mr. Davies explained. "From what we've gathered, it seems he was defending another student who was being bullied. However, things escalated quickly, and now both Liam and the other student are in trouble. The parents have been notified, and there's going to be a disciplinary hearing."

Jayden was stunned. Liam had always been quiet and kind; he couldn't imagine him getting into a fight. "But Liam was just trying to help," Jayden said, his voice tinged with disbelief. "He's not the type to start fights."

"I understand, Jayden," Mr. Davies said gently. "But the situation is complicated. Even though Liam's intentions may have been good, the school has a zero-tolerance policy when it comes to physical altercations. I'm telling you this because I know you're close to him, and I thought you should hear it from me first."

Jayden nodded slowly, trying to process the information. "Can I talk to him?"

Mr. Davies hesitated, then nodded. "I'll allow it, but you need to understand that this situation is serious. Liam is very upset, and he could use a friend right now."

Jayden thanked Mr. Davies and left the office, his mind racing. He couldn't believe that Liam was in such trouble. It didn't seem fair—Liam had only been trying to do the right thing. But as Jayden made his way to the room where Liam was waiting, he realized that this was exactly the kind of test he had been preparing for.

When Jayden entered the room, he found Liam sitting alone, his head in his hands. He looked up when Jayden walked in, and Jayden could see the anguish in his eyes.

"Liam," Jayden said softly, sitting down next to him. "What happened?"

Liam sighed; his voice shaky. "It all happened so fast. There was this kid, Alex, who was being picked on by a couple of older guys. I couldn't just stand there and do nothing, so I stepped in. I didn't mean for it to turn into a fight, but they wouldn't back off. Next thing I knew, it was chaos. I… I think I messed up, Jayden."

Jayden placed a hand on Liam's shoulder. "You didn't mess up. You did what you thought was right. But now we need to figure out how to handle this."

Liam looked down, his expression pained. "I don't know what to do. My parents are going to be so disappointed. And what if I get expelled? Everything's ruined."

Jayden felt a surge of determination. This was his chance to apply everything he had learned from the Quantum Path—to help Liam navigate this challenge in a way that reflected their values.

"Liam, listen to me," Jayden said firmly. "You made a tough call in a difficult situation. We can't change what happened, but we can figure out the best way to move forward. The important thing is that you're honest about what happened and why you did what you did."

Liam looked up, his eyes searching Jayden's. "But what if they don't believe me? What if they think I'm just another troublemaker?"

Jayden shook his head. "You're not a troublemaker, Liam. You're someone who stood up for what was right. And if we explain that to them, they'll understand. You're not alone in this—
I'll be there with you every step of the way."

Liam took a deep breath, nodding slowly. "Okay. I'll try."

As they left the room together, Jayden couldn't help but think about how this situation mirrored the challenges he had faced on his journey. Just like Liam, he had been faced with tough decisions, and he had learned that the right path wasn't always the easiest one. But with courage, honesty, and support, they could find a way through.

The next few days were a whirlwind of meetings with teachers, the principal, and Liam's parents. Jayden stood by his friend's side, helping him explain the situation and advocating for a fair outcome. It was stressful and exhausting, but Jayden never wavered. He knew that this was his ultimate test—not just of his own character, but of the lessons he had learned along the way.

In the end, the school decided that while Liam's actions had been against the rules, his intentions had been honorable. He was given a strict warning and assigned community service, but he was allowed to stay in school. It was a tough outcome, but it was far better than what Liam had feared.

As they walked home together after the final meeting, Liam turned to Jayden, gratitude shining in his eyes. "I don't know what I would have done without you, Jayden. You really helped me through this."

Jayden smiled, feeling a deep sense of accomplishment. "We helped each other, Liam. That's what friends are for."

Liam nodded, his expression serious. "I've learned a lot from this. Not just about standing up for what's right, but about facing the consequences, too. And I've learned that I can count on you, no matter what."

Jayden felt a warmth in his chest. This was what the Quantum Path had been preparing him for all along—to be someone who made a difference, not just in his own life, but in the lives of others.

As they parted ways, Jayden felt the familiar vibration of the device in his pocket. He pulled it out, curious to see what message it had for him this time.

"The greatest tests are not of strength, but of character. You have passed."

Jayden smiled as he put the device away. The ultimate test had come and gone, and he had emerged stronger, wiser, and more certain of his path than ever before

Chapter 11: The Power of Unity

With the events of Liam's ordeal behind them, Jayden found himself reflecting more deeply on the importance of the bonds he had forged with his friends. The challenge they had just faced had brought them closer together, and Jayden realized that their unity was one of the most powerful forces they had. But the Quantum Path still had more lessons to teach, and Jayden knew that their journey wasn't over yet.

One afternoon, Jayden, Emily, Kai, and Liam gathered at their favorite spot in the park—a secluded area near a small pond where they often went to talk and unwind. The atmosphere was peaceful, with the sun casting a warm glow over the water. But despite the serene setting, there was a sense of anticipation in the air, as if something important was about to happen.

Kai was the first to speak, breaking the comfortable silence. "You know, ever since we started on this journey together, I've been thinking a lot about what it means to be part of something bigger than myself. I used to think I could handle everything on my own, but now I see how much stronger we are when we're united."

Emily nodded in agreement. "Yeah, I feel the same way. We've all grown so much, and it's because we've had each other's backs through everything. It's like we're more than just friends now—we're a team."

Liam, who had been quietly gazing at the pond, looked up with a thoughtful expression. "I don't think I would have made it through the last few days without you guys. I've learned that I don't have to face things alone, and that's made all the difference."

Jayden listened to his friends, feeling a deep sense of connection with them. He had always known that they were important to him, but now he understood just how essential their unity was. The Quantum Path wasn't just about individual growth; it was about learning to work together, to support each other, and to draw strength from their collective bond.

As if in response to their conversation, the device in Jayden's pocket began to vibrate. He pulled it out, and the others gathered around, eager to see what new message it had for them.

"When individuals unite, they form a force greater than the sum of their parts. Embrace the power of unity, and you will achieve the extraordinary."

Jayden read the message aloud, and the group exchanged knowing looks. The message resonated deeply with all of them, confirming what they had just been discussing.

Emily smiled, her eyes sparkling with determination. "I think it's time we put this to the test. We've been learning all these lessons, but what if we used what we've learned to take on something bigger—something that could really make a difference?"

Kai grinned, clearly excited by the idea. "I'm in. But what exactly do you have in mind?"

Emily's smile widened. "I've been thinking about that. There's this environmental issue that's been bothering me for a while—the park we're in now, it's under threat of being developed into a commercial area. A lot of people in the community don't want it to happen, but they feel powerless to stop it. What if we used what we've learned to help?"

Jayden felt a surge of inspiration at Emily's words. The park was a special place for them, a sanctuary where they had shared so many important moments. The thought of it being destroyed for commercial gain filled him with a sense of purpose.

"That's a great idea, Emily," Jayden said, his voice filled with resolve. "We've learned that we can create ripples with our actions, so let's use those ripples to protect this place. We can organize the community, raise awareness, and show everyone that we're stronger together."

Liam, who had been listening intently, nodded. "It's not just about saving the park—it's about showing people that they have the power to make a difference. We can be the ones to start that movement."

The group spent the next few days planning their strategy. They reached out to local activists, created flyers, and started a social media campaign to rally support. It wasn't long before their efforts began to gain traction, and more and more people joined their cause.

Jayden was amazed by how quickly things started to come together. People from all walks of life showed up at their meetings, eager to help protect the park. The energy in the community was palpable, and Jayden realized that their unity had created something truly powerful— a movement that couldn't be ignored.

As the campaign gained momentum, Jayden and his friends found themselves facing new challenges. There were moments of doubt, times when it seemed like the forces against them were too strong. But each time, they reminded themselves of the lessons they had learned from the Quantum Path.

They remembered the power of perseverance, the importance of standing up for what was right, and the strength they drew from each other. And as they faced each obstacle together, their bond grew even stronger.

The culmination of their efforts came on the day of the city council meeting, where the decision about the park's future would be made. Jayden, Emily, Kai, and Liam stood at the front of the packed room, ready to present their case.

Jayden took a deep breath, feeling a mixture of nerves and determination. This was it—the moment when everything they had worked for would be put to the test. He looked at his friends, and they all nodded in silent support.

When it was Jayden's turn to speak, he stepped up to the podium and began to tell their story. He spoke about the lessons they had learned, the unity they had forged, and the power of coming together for a common cause. As he spoke, he could see the faces of the council members softening, their expressions changing from skepticism to understanding.

Jayden concluded his speech with words that came straight from the heart. "This park isn't just a piece of land—it's a place where people come together, where memories are made, and where our community can thrive. We've learned that when we unite, we can achieve the extraordinary. And we believe that together, we can protect this place for future generations." The room erupted in applause, and Jayden felt a surge of hope. The council members exchanged glances, clearly moved by the passion and unity they had witnessed.

After what felt like an eternity, the council announced their decision: the park would be preserved.

Cheers filled the room, and Jayden and his friends hugged each other, overwhelmed with relief and joy. They had done it. They had come together, used everything they had learned, and made a real difference.

As they left the meeting, the device in Jayden's pocket vibrated once more. He pulled it out, eager to see the final message.

"Unity is the key to unlocking the extraordinary. You have harnessed its power and changed your world."

Jayden smiled as he shared the message with his friends. They had truly embraced the power of unity, and in doing so, they had achieved something extraordinary.

As they walked through the park, now safe from development, Jayden felt a deep sense of fulfillment. The Quantum Path had taught them many things, but perhaps the most important lesson was that they were stronger together.

Chapter 12: The Quantum Choice

The victory of saving the park filled Jayden and his friends with a renewed sense of purpose and unity. They had accomplished something meaningful, proving to themselves and the community that change was possible when people came together. However, Jayden knew that their journey on the Quantum Path was not over. There was still one final lesson, one final test that would challenge everything they had learned.

A few weeks after the city council meeting, Jayden began to notice strange occurrences—small anomalies that seemed to defy logic. It started with minor things, like objects shifting positions without explanation or brief flashes of light in the corner of his eye. At first, he dismissed them as coincidences or tricks of the mind, but as they became more frequent, Jayden grew concerned.

One evening, as Jayden was lying in bed, the device in his pocket started vibrating more intensely than ever before. He pulled it out, expecting the usual message, but this time, the device projected a shimmering hologram into the air above him. The hologram displayed a swirling vortex of light, and Jayden's heart raced as he watched it.

Suddenly, the vortex expanded, and Jayden found himself enveloped in its glow. The room around him faded away, and he felt as though he were floating in an infinite space of light and energy. A voice, calm and resonant, echoed in his mind.

"Jayden, you have reached the final stage of your journey. The Quantum Path has prepared you for this moment. But now, you must make a choice—a choice that will determine your future and the future of those around you."

Jayden felt a mixture of awe and trepidation. "What choice do I have to make?" he asked, his voice trembling slightly.

The voice continued, its tone both reassuring and serious. **"The Quantum Path has shown you the power of unity, the importance of perseverance, and the strength of character. Now, you must decide how to use this knowledge. You have the opportunity to embrace the Quantum Path fully, to become a guardian of its wisdom and use it to guide others. However, this choice comes with great responsibility and sacrifice. You may also choose to return to your normal life, carrying the lessons with you but without the burden of guardianship. The choice is yours."**

Jayden's mind raced as he tried to process the magnitude of the decision before him. The idea of becoming a guardian of the Quantum Path was both exhilarating and daunting. He had learned so much, and the thought of using that knowledge to help others was deeply appealing. But he also knew that it would come with significant sacrifices—his life would never be the same.

As he floated in the vortex of light, Jayden thought about his friends, his family, and everything he had experienced. He thought about the challenges they had faced together, the lives they had touched, and the impact they had made. He realized that whatever choice he made, it would not only affect him but also those he cared about.

The voice spoke again, gently urging him to decide. **"Your journey has brought you to this moment. Trust in what you have learned, and choose the path that aligns with your true self."**

Jayden closed his eyes, taking a deep breath. He knew that this was the moment he had been preparing for, the culmination of everything he had learned on the Quantum Path. He could feel the weight of the decision pressing down on him, but he also felt a sense of clarity—a knowing that whatever choice he made, it would be the right one for him.

After what felt like an eternity, Jayden opened his eyes and spoke with quiet resolve. "I choose to embrace the Quantum Path fully. I choose to be a guardian, to use what I've learned to guide and protect others. I know it won't be easy, but I believe this is the path I'm meant to follow."

As soon as the words left his mouth, the vortex of light intensified, surrounding Jayden in a cocoon of energy. The voice, now filled with warmth and approval, spoke one final time.

"Your choice is made, and the Quantum Path welcomes you as a guardian.

You will carry its wisdom and light, guiding others on their journeys. Remember, the path ahead is one of service, but it is also one of profound fulfillment. Go forth, Jayden, and may the light of the Quantum Path always be with you."

The light around Jayden began to fade, and he felt himself gently returning to his bed. When he opened his eyes, he was back in his room, the device in his hand now glowing with a soft, steady light. He felt a deep sense of peace, as though a great weight had been lifted from his shoulders.

The next day, Jayden shared his experience with his friends. They listened with awe and respect, understanding the significance of the choice he had made. While they couldn't fully grasp what it meant to be a guardian of the Quantum Path, they knew that Jayden's journey was far from over.

Emily, always the practical one, smiled and said, "You've chosen a path that not many would have the courage to take, Jayden. But we'll be here for you, just like we always have been."

Kai nodded; his expression serious. "You're going to do amazing things, Jayden.

I'm sure of it. And whatever comes next, we're in this together."

Liam, who had grown so much since his own ordeal, added, "I think this is just the beginning. The Quantum Path brought us together for a reason, and maybe there's still more for us to do."

Jayden looked at his friends, feeling a deep sense of gratitude and connection. "I wouldn't have been able to make this choice without you guys. You've been with me through everything, and I know that we're stronger together. Whatever the future holds, we'll face it as a team."

As they sat together in the park, the same place where their journey had begun, Jayden felt a profound sense of purpose. He knew that the path ahead would be challenging, but he also knew that it was the right one for him. He was ready to embrace his role as a guardian of the Quantum Path, and he was ready to continue making a difference in the world.

The journey was far from over, but Jayden felt confident that he was exactly where he was meant to be.

Chapter 13: A New Dawn

After making the monumental decision to embrace the Quantum Path fully, Jayden found his life taking on a new rhythm. The days that followed were filled with a sense of purpose and calm, but also a growing awareness that his journey as a guardian was only just beginning. The device that had guided him through so much now served as a constant reminder of the path he had chosen—a path that would require him to step into a new role, not just for himself, but for others as well.

One morning, Jayden awoke with a feeling of anticipation, as if something significant was about to happen. The sun had barely risen, casting a gentle light over his room, and the air was filled with the quiet stillness that comes before a new day truly begins. Jayden got out of bed and dressed quickly, his mind racing with thoughts of what lay ahead.

He didn't have to wait long for a sign. As he was preparing to leave his room, the device in his pocket began to vibrate softly, signaling a new message. Jayden pulled it out, and as the familiar light enveloped him, a message appeared:

"A new dawn brings new challenges. Your journey as a guardian begins today. Trust in the lessons you have learned, and remember that the path of service is one of both guidance and protection. You are not alone."

Jayden read the message with a sense of calm determination. He knew that this day would mark the start of his true role as a guardian, and he was ready to embrace whatever came his way. With the message still fresh in his mind, he headed out to meet his friends.

They had agreed to meet at the park, the place that had become their sanctuary and the symbol of their unity. When Jayden arrived, he found Emily, Kai, and Liam already there, waiting for him. There was an unspoken understanding among them—they knew that today was different, that something significant was about to begin.

Emily was the first to speak, her voice filled with quiet confidence. "I've been thinking a lot about what you told us, Jayden. About being a guardian of the Quantum Path. I think we all have a role to play in this, even if it's different from yours."

Kai nodded in agreement. "We've been through so much together, and I feel like we're all part of something bigger now. Maybe we're not guardians in the same way you are, Jayden, but we're still in this with you. We can help you protect and guide others."

Liam, who had grown more confident and sure of himself over the course of their journey, added, "I don't think we would have made it this far if we hadn't learned to rely on each other. Whatever comes next, we'll face it together. That's what being a team is all about."

Jayden felt a deep sense of gratitude as he listened to his friends. They had been with him every step of the way, and now, they were ready to stand by his side as he stepped into his new role. He knew that being a guardian wasn't something he could do alone—it was something that would require the strength and unity of his entire team.

With this in mind, Jayden took a deep breath and began to speak. "You're right. We've been through so much together, and I couldn't have come this far without you. The Quantum Path has shown me that true strength comes from unity, and that's something we've always had.

As a guardian, I'm going to need your help—your support, your wisdom, and your strength. We're in this together, just like we always have been."

Emily smiled, her eyes shining with determination. "Then let's do this. Whatever challenges come our way, we'll face them as a team. The Quantum Path brought us together for a reason, and I believe we're meant to use what we've learned to help others."

Kai grinned, his usual enthusiasm bubbling to the surface. "We've got this. We've faced everything from time loops to saving the park, and we've come out stronger each time. Let's see what else the Quantum Path has in store for us."

Liam, who had once been the quietest of the group, now spoke with a newfound confidence. "We've learned so much, and now it's our turn to give back. We can make a difference, just like we did with the park. This is just the beginning."

As they stood together in the early morning light, Jayden felt a profound sense of connection to his friends and to the path they had chosen. The Quantum Path had brought them together, taught them valuable lessons, and now it was guiding them into a new phase of their journey— one where they would use their knowledge to help others.

Suddenly, the device in Jayden's pocket began to glow, not with a message this time, but with a bright, steady light that seemed to pulse with energy. The light grew brighter and brighter until it surrounded all four of them, lifting them into a state of heightened awareness. In that moment, they felt as though they were connected to something far greater than themselves— a vast network of energy and wisdom that spanned across time and space.

As the light faded, they found themselves standing in the park, but it felt different now, as if it had been infused with a new sense of purpose. Jayden looked at his friends and saw that they had all felt the same thing—that they were now part of something much larger than they had ever imagined.

The day passed quickly as they discussed their next steps. They knew that their new roles would require them to be vigilant, to look out for signs that others might need their help, and to be ready to act when the time came. But they also knew that they didn't have to do it alone— they had each other, and they had the wisdom of the Quantum Path to guide them.

As the sun began to set, casting a warm glow over the park, Jayden felt a deep sense of peace. He knew that this was just the beginning of a new chapter in their lives, one that would be filled with challenges, but also with incredible opportunities to make a difference. And with his friends by his side, he was ready to face whatever the future held.

Chapter 14: The Guardians' First Mission

The transition into their new roles as guardians of the Quantum Path was both exciting and daunting for Jayden and his friends. The park, which had been the backdrop for many of their previous adventures, now felt like a place of both comfort and responsibility. They knew that their journey had shifted into something more significant—something that required them to be vigilant and ready to act.

Days turned into weeks, and the group began to settle into their new roles. They kept their eyes open for signs of people in need, quietly observing the world around them for any indication that the Quantum Path was calling them to action. Jayden, especially, felt the weight of his decision to embrace the role of a guardian. The responsibility was immense, but so was the sense of purpose that came with it.

One afternoon, as they were walking through the park discussing their day, the device in Jayden's pocket suddenly vibrated. He pulled it out, and a new message appeared on the screen, causing the group to stop in their tracks.

"A new challenge arises. Seek out those who are lost, guide them to the light, and protect them from the shadows. Your first mission as guardians begins now."

The message was clear, yet mysterious. The group exchanged glances, feeling a mix of excitement and apprehension. This was it—the moment they had been preparing for.

Emily was the first to break the silence. "We need to figure out where we're supposed to go. The message says to seek out those who are lost. But who are they? And where do we find them?"

Kai, always eager to jump into action, suggested, "Maybe we should start by exploring areas we don't usually go to. If someone is lost, they're probably somewhere unfamiliar or isolated."

Jayden nodded thoughtfully. "That makes sense. We need to keep our minds open and trust that the Quantum Path will guide us. Let's split up and cover more ground. If any of us find something, we can contact the others."

The group agreed and decided to split into pairs—Jayden with Emily and Kai with Liam. They would search different parts of the city, focusing on places where people might be struggling or in need of help.

Jayden and Emily headed toward the older part of town, where the buildings were worn and the streets less traveled. As they walked, they kept their senses sharp, looking for any sign that might lead them to those who were lost. The area was quiet, almost eerily so, with only a few people passing by, most of them hurrying along with their heads down.

As they turned down a narrow alleyway, Jayden noticed something strange. A faint, shimmering light seemed to flicker at the edge of his vision. He stopped in his tracks, narrowing his eyes as he tried to focus on it.

"Do you see that?" Jayden asked Emily, pointing toward the source of the light.

Emily squinted, then nodded. "Yeah, I see it. It's like a glow, but it's not coming from any light source I can see. Do you think it's connected to the Quantum Path?"

Jayden felt a surge of certainty. "I think it is. Let's follow it."

They moved cautiously toward the light, which seemed to grow stronger as they approached. It led them deeper into the alley until they came to a small courtyard that was hidden from the main street. The courtyard was empty, except for a single figure sitting on a bench, hunched over and surrounded by an aura of the shimmering light.

As they got closer, they could see that it was a young man, probably in his early twenties, with a troubled expression on his face. He looked up as they approached, his eyes filled with confusion and fear.

"Who are you?" the young man asked, his voice shaky. "And how did you find me?"

Jayden stepped forward, his tone gentle and reassuring. "My name is Jayden, and this is Emily. We're here to help you. We followed the light—your light. You don't have to be afraid."

The young man looked at them with a mixture of hope and skepticism. "I don't know what's happening. I've been feeling… lost, like I'm not sure where I'm supposed to be or what I'm supposed to do. And then this strange light started following me. I thought I was going crazy." Emily smiled kindly. "You're not crazy. The light is a sign that you're connected to something greater, something that's trying to guide you. We've been sent to help you find your way."

The young man hesitated, then nodded slowly. "I've been struggling with a lot of things lately—my job, my family, my purpose in life. It feels like everything is falling apart, and I don't know how to fix it."

Jayden could see the pain in his eyes and felt a deep sense of compassion. "You're not alone in this. We've all been through moments where we felt lost and unsure of what to do. But you've already taken the first step by reaching out, even if you didn't realize it. The Quantum Path led us to you because it knows you're ready to find your way."

The young man seemed to relax slightly, as if a burden had been lifted from his shoulders. "What do I need to do?"

Emily spoke softly. "First, take a deep breath and try to clear your mind. Let go of the fear and confusion for just a moment. Then, focus on what you truly want in life—the things that matter most to you."

The young man closed his eyes and took a few deep breaths. Jayden and Emily stood quietly, giving him space to center himself. After a few moments, the young man opened his eyes, a look of determination replacing the fear.

"I want to find a way to make a difference," he said, his voice steady. "I want to help others who are struggling, just like I've been. I want to be someone who brings light to others, instead of just feeling lost in the dark."

Jayden smiled, feeling a sense of fulfilment. "That's a noble goal, and it's something you're more than capable of achieving. The Quantum Path will continue to guide you, but you have to trust yourself and take the steps toward the life you want."

The young man nodded, a spark of hope in his eyes. "Thank you. I feel like I've found a direction now, like I'm not just drifting anymore."

As they spoke, the shimmering light around the young man began to fade, leaving behind a calm, peaceful glow. It was a sign that he had found his way, at least for now.

Jayden and Emily exchanged a look of satisfaction, knowing that they had successfully completed their first mission as guardians. They walked the young man back to the main street, giving him words of encouragement before parting ways. As they headed back to the park to meet up with Kai and Liam, Jayden and Emily couldn't help but feel a deep sense of accomplishment. Their first mission had not only tested their abilities as guardians but also reaffirmed the importance of their roles. They had helped someone find his way out of the darkness, and in doing so, they had taken their first steps toward fulfilling their responsibilities as protectors of the Quantum Path.

When they arrived at the park, they found Kai and Liam waiting for them, both looking eager to hear about what had happened.

"So, did you guys find anything?" Kai asked, his eyes full of curiosity.

Jayden nodded, a smile on his face. "We did. We found someone who was lost—someone who needed guidance. The Quantum Path led us to him, and we helped him find a new sense of direction in his life."

Liam grinned. "That's awesome! We didn't find anything as dramatic, but we did notice a few places where people seemed to be struggling. We talked to a few of them, offered some support. It feels good to help, even in small ways."

Emily added, "It's clear that the Quantum Path is guiding us to those who need our help. We just have to stay alert and be ready to step in when the time comes."

Kai looked thoughtful. "I guess that's what being a guardian is all about—being there for people, guiding them when they're lost, and protecting them from the shadows. It's a big responsibility, but it feels right."

Jayden agreed, feeling a deep sense of unity with his friends. "We're just getting started, but I think we're on the right track. The Quantum Path has brought us together for a reason, and as long as we trust in that, we'll be able to make a real difference."

As they sat together in the park, the sun setting behind them, the group felt a renewed sense of purpose. They knew that their journey as guardians was just beginning and that there would be many more challenges ahead. But with each mission, they were growing stronger, more connected to each other, and more attuned to the Quantum Path.

The night settled in, casting long shadows across the park, but the light within them—ignited by their shared purpose—burned brightly. They were ready to face whatever came next, together.

Chapter 15: Shadows in the Light

After their first successful mission as guardians, Jayden and his friends felt more confident in their abilities. Each day, they honed their skills, deepening their connection to the Quantum Path, and becoming more attuned to the subtle energies around them. The park remained their base, a place where they could regroup, reflect, and plan their next steps. But as they grew stronger, so too did the challenges they faced.

One evening, as the group was gathered in the park, the atmosphere shifted. The air, usually filled with the sounds of birds and rustling leaves, became heavy with an eerie stillness. Jayden felt a chill run down his spine, and he noticed that the light in the park seemed dimmer, as if something was draining the energy around them.

Kai, always quick to notice when something was off, looked around nervously. "Do you guys feel that? It's like the whole park just got darker. I don't like this."

Emily nodded, her eyes narrowing as she scanned their surroundings. "Something's not right. We should be on our guard."

Liam, who had become more attuned to the energies of the Quantum Path, closed his eyes and focused. "I can sense it too. There's something here, something... dark. It feels like it's watching us."

Jayden took a deep breath, trying to centre himself. "Stay close, everyone. We don't know what we're dealing with yet, but we're stronger together."

As they huddled closer, the device in Jayden's pocket began to vibrate, signalling a new message. He pulled it out, and a message appeared on the screen, the words glowing faintly against the dim light:

"Beware the shadows. Not all who walk in the light have pure intentions. Trust in your bond, and protect each other from those who would seek to harm you."

The warning sent a shiver through the group. They had encountered challenges before, but this felt different—more personal, more dangerous. The Quantum Path was alerting them to a threat that they couldn't see, but one that was clearly present.

Kai clenched his fists, his usual bravado giving way to concern. "So, there's something—or someone—out there that's trying to mess with us? We've handled tough situations before, but this feels... sinister."

Emily, ever the strategist, tried to think through their options. "If the Quantum Path is warning us, then whatever it is must be close. We need to be careful. We can't afford to let our guard down."

Liam opened his eyes, a look of determination on his face. "Whatever this is, we'll face it together. We've come too far to back down now."

Just as they were about to discuss their next move, a figure stepped out from behind one of the large trees at the edge of the park. The person was cloaked in darkness, their face obscured by the shadows that seemed to cling to them. The group instinctively took a step back, sensing the danger that emanated from the stranger.

The figure spoke, their voice low and menacing. "So, you're the ones who've been meddling with the Quantum Path. I've been watching you, waiting for the right moment to introduce myself."

Jayden stood his ground, feeling the weight of his responsibility as a guardian. "Who are you? And what do you want from us?"

The figure chuckled, the sound sending a cold wave through the group. "Who I am isn't important. What matters is that you've been interfering with things you don't fully understand. The Quantum Path is not just a force for good—it's a power, and power attracts those who seek to control it."

Emily stepped forward, her voice steady. "We're not trying to control anything. We're here to help those in need, to protect and guide others along the path."

The figure's eyes glinted in the dim light, a predatory look in their gaze. "Noble words, but naïve. The Quantum Path is much more than you realize, and there are those who will do whatever it takes to claim its power. If you continue on this path, you'll find yourselves up against forces far beyond your comprehension."

Jayden felt a surge of defiance. "We're not afraid of you, or anyone else who tries to threaten us. We're stronger than you think."

The figure's smile was cold and mocking. "We'll see about that. Consider this your first and only warning. Stay out of my way, or you'll regret it."

With that, the figure melted back into the shadows, disappearing as quickly as they had appeared. The darkness that had settled over the park began to lift, but the sense of unease remained.

Kai let out a breath he hadn't realized he was holding. "What was that about? Who was that guy?"

Emily shook her head, her expression troubled. "I don't know, but whoever he is, he's dangerous. We need to be prepared for whatever comes next."

Liam looked at Jayden, concern etched on his face. "Do you think he's right? That we're dealing with something we don't fully understand?"

Jayden didn't hesitate. "Maybe we don't understand everything yet, but we've come this far because we trust in the Quantum Path and in each other. We can't let fear stop us now."

The group nodded in agreement, though the encounter had clearly shaken them. They knew that their journey as guardians had just become more complicated and that the stakes were higher than ever.

As they walked out of the park, their minds were filled with thoughts of the mysterious figure and the warning he had given them. The Quantum Path had always been a source of guidance and light, but now they were beginning to see that it could also attract darkness—and that darkness was something they would have to face.

Chapter 16: A Fracture in the Team

The warning from the shadowy figure hung over the group like a dark cloud. Despite their determination, Jayden and his friends couldn't shake the unease that had settled in. The encounter had not only introduced a new threat but had also planted seeds of doubt among them.

Over the next few days, the group continued their efforts to help those in need, but the tension was palpable. Kai, usually the most carefree of the group, was uncharacteristically quiet. Emily, the planner, seemed more cautious than usual, second-guessing her decisions. Liam, always the calm and thoughtful one, appeared distracted, as if something was weighing heavily on his mind.

Jayden noticed these changes but struggled to find a way to address them. He knew that the strength of their team lay in their unity, but the encounter with the mysterious figure had clearly shaken that foundation. As their leader, he felt a responsibility to bring them back together, but he wasn't sure how.

One afternoon, as they gathered in the park to discuss their next move, the underlying tension finally boiled over.

"I've been thinking," Kai began, breaking the uneasy silence. "Maybe that guy was right. Maybe we don't fully understand what we're getting ourselves into. We've been so focused on helping others that we haven't stopped to consider the risks."

Emily frowned, her voice defensive. "What are you saying, Kai? That we should just give up because we're scared? We knew from the beginning that this wasn't going to be easy."

Kai shook his head, frustration evident in his tone. "I'm not saying we should give up. But we need to be smart about this. We can't just charge ahead blindly. We need to know what we're up against."

Liam, who had been silent up to this point, finally spoke up, his voice quiet but firm. "Kai has a point. We've been reacting to things as they happen, but we need to be more proactive. We need to understand the Quantum Path better, and we need to figure out who that guy was and what he wants."

Jayden listened to his friends, feeling the weight of their words. They were all making valid points, but he could sense the fear and uncertainty underlying their arguments. He knew that if they didn't address these feelings, it could tear their team apart.

"Look," Jayden said, trying to keep his voice calm and steady, "I get that we're all worried. What happened with that guy was a wake-up call. But we can't let fear control us. We've faced challenges before, and we've always come out stronger because we trust each other and the Quantum Path."

Emily crossed her arms, her expression troubled. "It's not just about trust, Jayden. It's about being prepared. We don't even know what the Quantum Path really is, or why it chose us. We need answers."

Kai nodded in agreement. "Yeah, and we need to know more about the dangers out there. If we don't, we could be walking into a trap."

Jayden felt a pang of frustration. He understood their concerns, but he also knew that dwelling on fear could paralyze them. They needed to find a way to move forward without letting their doubts consume them.

"Okay," Jayden said, taking a deep breath. "You're right—we need more information. So, let's figure out how to get it. Maybe we can start by looking into the history of the Quantum Path, see if we can find any clues about what we're dealing with. And we should also keep an eye out for any signs of that guy or anyone else who might be a threat."

Liam nodded thoughtfully. "That's a good start. We need to approach this logically, not just with emotion. If we can gather more information, we'll be better equipped to handle whatever comes our way."

Emily's expression softened slightly, and she nodded in agreement. "I think that's a good plan.

We can't afford to be caught off guard again."

Kai looked relieved, the tension in his shoulders easing. "Yeah, I can get behind that. We've been through too much to let this break us."

Jayden felt a sense of relief as well. They were still on edge, but at least they were talking things through. He knew that this was a crucial moment for their team, a test of their unity and resolve.

"Alright," Jayden said, his voice firm. "Let's start by doing some research. We'll split up and see what we can find out about the Quantum Path and any potential threats. And if anyone sees or hears anything suspicious, we share it immediately. We're in this together, and that's how we'll get through it."

The group agreed, their resolve strengthening as they discussed their next steps. The fracture that had begun to form in their team was still there, but it was starting to mend. Jayden knew that they still had a lot of work to do, both in terms of their mission and in rebuilding the trust that had been shaken. But for now, they were moving forward, and that was what mattered.

As they left the park, Jayden couldn't help but feel a mixture of hope and trepidation. The road ahead was uncertain, and the shadows that lurked in the corners of their journey were growing darker. But he knew that as long as they stuck together, they could face whatever came their way.

Chapter 17: The Search for Answers

Determined to uncover more about the Quantum Path and the mysterious figure who had threatened them, Jayden and his friends split up to do some serious digging. The park, once a place of comfort, now felt more like a war room where they strategized and planned their every move.

Jayden decided to start by visiting the town's library, a place he hadn't frequented much before this whole adventure began. He hoped to find some historical records or texts that might shed light on the Quantum Path. Kai, who had a knack for technology, took it upon himself to search the internet and online forums for any mention of the Quantum Path or similar phenomena. Emily and Liam opted to explore the more spiritual side, visiting a local metaphysical shop that was known for its collection of rare books and artifacts.

As Jayden walked into the library, the scent of old books filled his senses. It was quiet, save for the occasional rustle of pages or the soft footsteps of other visitors. He headed straight to the history section, figuring that if the Quantum Path had been around for a long time, there might be some record of it buried in the past.

Hours passed as Jayden combed through book after book, but nothing seemed to directly reference the Quantum Path. He found mentions of ancient spiritual practices, energy fields, and even some local legends about mysterious forces, but nothing concrete. Frustration began to creep in, but he knew he couldn't give up. The answer had to be out there somewhere.

Meanwhile, Kai was hunched over his laptop at a local café, his fingers flying across the keyboard as he sifted through countless websites, forums, and online communities. He was amazed at how many people were out there searching for answers to strange occurrences, unexplained phenomena, and mystical experiences. But like Jayden, he struggled to find anything that directly mentioned the Quantum Path.

After several hours of digging, Kai stumbled upon a post in a forgotten corner of a conspiracy theory forum. The post was old, dated nearly ten years ago, and it was written by someone who claimed to have encountered a "force" that guided people toward their true purpose. The description was vague, but it resonated with what Kai and his friends had experienced. He quickly bookmarked the page and made a note to share it with the group later.

Emily and Liam were having better luck at the metaphysical shop. The place was filled with crystals, incense, and all sorts of spiritual paraphernalia. The shop's owner, an older woman with a kind smile and deep knowledge of all things mystical, was more than happy to help them.

"You're looking for information on the Quantum Path, you say?" the woman asked, her eyes twinkling with curiosity. "That's not a term I've heard in quite some time. It's an ancient concept, often associated with the idea of destiny or a higher calling. It's said that those who walk the Quantum Path are chosen to fulfill a special purpose, one that can change the course of history."

Liam's eyes widened. "So it's real? The Quantum Path isn't just something we imagined?"

The woman nodded. "Oh, it's very real, though it's not something most people are aware of. The Quantum Path is believed to be a guiding force, one that helps those who are meant to make a difference find their way. But it's not without its dangers. There are always those who would seek to use such power for their own gain."

Emily leaned forward, eager to learn more. "We encountered someone who seemed to know about the Quantum Path. He wasn't friendly, and he warned us to stay out of his way. Do you know who he might be?"

The woman's expression darkened slightly. "There are stories, of course. Legends of those who have tried to control the Quantum Path, to bend it to their will. Such people are dangerous, not just because of their knowledge, but because they've lost sight of what the Path is truly about. They see it as a tool, a means to an end, rather than a sacred journey."

Liam exchanged a glance with Emily. "Do you have any books or anything that could help us understand more about this?"

The woman thought for a moment before nodding. "I do have something that might help. It's an old manuscript, not widely known, but it contains information about the Quantum Path and those who have walked it before. It's not a complete guide, but it might provide you with some of the answers you're looking for."

She disappeared into a back room, returning a few moments later with a small, leather-bound book. The cover was worn, and the pages were yellowed with age. Emily took it carefully, feeling the weight of its significance.

"Thank you," she said, her voice full of gratitude.

The woman smiled. "Use it wisely. The Quantum Path is a gift, but it requires wisdom and courage to walk it. Be careful, and trust in your bond with each other. That's your greatest strength."

As Emily and Liam left the shop, they couldn't help but feel a renewed sense of purpose. They had found a lead, something that might help them understand the Quantum Path better and prepare for the challenges ahead.

That evening, the group reconvened at the park, each of them sharing what they had discovered. Jayden's frustration faded as he listened to Emily and Liam talk about the manuscript, and Kai's discovery on the forum provided another piece of the puzzle.

"Sounds like we've got some reading to do," Jayden said, holding up the manuscript. "If this can give us even a hint about what we're dealing with, it'll be worth it."

Kai grinned. "And I'll keep digging online. There's bound to be more out there that we haven't found yet."

Emily nodded. "And we should stay vigilant. The woman at the shop was clear—there are those who would use the Quantum Path for their own purposes. We can't let our guard down."

Liam added, "But we also need to remember why we're doing this. We're here to help, to guide, and to protect. That's what makes us different from those who seek to control the Path."

Jayden felt a sense of unity returning to the group. The shadows that had begun to divide them were starting to dissipate, replaced by a renewed determination to see their mission through.

"Let's get to work," Jayden said, and the group nodded in agreement, ready to continue their journey along the Quantum Path—together.

Chapter 18: The Trial of the Guardians

Armed with new knowledge from the ancient manuscript and Kai's online discovery, Jayden and his friends were more determined than ever to fulfill their roles as guardians of the Quantum Path. But they knew their journey was far from over—if anything, the real challenges were just beginning.

The manuscript spoke of an ancient trial, a rite of passage that all guardians had to undergo to prove their worth and solidify their connection to the Quantum Path. The trial was described as both a test of skill and character, designed to push each guardian to their limits. It was said that those who completed the trial emerged stronger, with a deeper understanding of the Path and their place within it.

One evening, as they gathered in the park to discuss their next steps, the device that had guided them so far began to emit a soft, pulsing light. Jayden pulled it out, and a new message appeared on the screen:

"The time has come to prove yourselves. Seek the Trial of the Guardians and face your fears. Only then will you unlock the true potential of the Quantum Path."

The message filled the group with a mix of excitement and anxiety. They had been preparing for this moment, but the reality of what lay ahead was daunting.

"So, it's finally happening," Kai said, trying to sound confident, though a hint of nervousness crept into his voice. "We've been training for this, right? We can handle it."

Emily, ever the strategist, nodded. "We've faced plenty of challenges before, but this… This is different. We need to be ready for anything. The manuscript mentioned that the trial would test us in ways we can't predict."

Liam, who had always been the group's voice of reason, spoke up. "Whatever happens, we need to remember that we're in this together. The Quantum Path has always been about our connection to each other. If we stick together, we'll get through this."

Jayden looked at his friends, feeling a surge of pride and affection. They had come so far together, and despite the obstacles they had faced, they were stronger than ever. "We've got this. No matter what the trial throws at us, we'll face it as a team."

The group agreed, their resolve solidified. The manuscript provided them with a clue about where the trial would take place—a location deep within the forest that bordered the town. It was said to be a place where the boundaries between the physical world and the Quantum Path were thin, allowing for powerful energies to manifest.

The next day, the group set out for the forest, following the directions in the manuscript. The deeper they ventured, the more the atmosphere around them seemed to change. The air grew cooler, and the light filtering through the trees took on an ethereal quality, as if the forest itself was alive with the energy of the Quantum Path.

After hours of trekking, they finally reached a clearing. In the center of the clearing stood an ancient stone structure, partially overgrown with vines and moss. The structure seemed out of place in the otherwise wild forest, as if it had been deliberately placed there long ago.

"This must be it," Emily said, her voice hushed with awe. "The Trial of the Guardians."

As they approached the structure, the device in Jayden's pocket began to pulse more rapidly, confirming that they were in the right place. The group stood in a circle around the structure, each of them feeling the weight of what was about to happen.

Suddenly, the ground beneath them began to tremble, and a blinding light erupted from the center of the structure. The light enveloped each of them, pulling them into a different realm— a realm that was both familiar and alien, a place where the rules of reality seemed to bend and twist.

Jayden found himself standing alone in a vast, empty space. The air around him was thick with energy, and he could feel the presence of the Quantum Path all around him. But something was off—there was a sense of foreboding, as if the very essence of the place was testing him.

A voice echoed through the void, deep and resonant. "Jayden, leader of the guardians, you have been chosen to face the Trial of Courage. Confront your greatest fear and emerge victorious, or be consumed by it."

Jayden's heart raced as the space around him began to shift. He was suddenly back in the park, but it was different—darker, more sinister. Shadows flickered at the edges of his vision, and the familiar comfort of the park was replaced by a sense of dread.

As he looked around, he saw figures emerging from the shadows— figures that looked like his friends, but distorted, twisted versions of them. They sneered at him, their eyes filled with malice.

"You think you're a leader?" one of the figures taunted, its voice a twisted version of Kai's. "You're weak, Jayden. You can't protect anyone."

Another figure, this one resembling Emily, stepped forward. "You're a failure, Jayden. You'll never be able to keep us safe."

Jayden felt a wave of fear and self-doubt wash over him. These were his deepest insecurities, the fears he had tried to bury for so long. But now they were manifesting before him, challenging his very sense of self.

For a moment, he felt himself start to waver. The voices of the twisted figures grew louder, their words cutting deep. But then he remembered his friends—the real Kai, Emily, and Liam. They believed in him, and they had stood by his side through everything. They saw something in him that he sometimes struggled to see in himself.

Taking a deep breath, Jayden steadied himself. "You're not real," he said, his voice firm.
"You're just my fears, nothing more. And I won't let you control me."

The figures snarled, their forms flickering as if they were losing their grip on reality. Jayden stepped forward, his fear turning into determination. "I'm not perfect, but I'm not weak either. I've made mistakes, but I've also grown because of them. And I won't let my fear define me."

With those words, the figures began to dissolve, their taunts fading into the void. The darkness around Jayden lifted, and he found himself back in the vast, empty space. The voice echoed once more, this time with a note of approval. "You have passed the Trial of Courage, Jayden. You are stronger than your fears."

As the light enveloped him again, Jayden felt a surge of power and confidence. He had faced his darkest fears and emerged victorious. He was ready for whatever lay ahead.

Elsewhere, his friends were undergoing their own trials, each of them confronting their deepest fears and insecurities. Kai faced a Trial of Loyalty, where he was tempted to abandon his friends in favor of an easier path. Emily faced a Trial of Wisdom, where she had to choose between what was right and what was easy. Liam faced a Trial of Faith, where he was forced to question everything he believed in.

One by one, they each overcame their trials, emerging stronger and more united than ever. When they finally reunited in the clearing, there was a sense of accomplishment and renewal among them. They had been tested in ways they had never imagined, but they had come through it together.

Jayden looked at his friends, feeling an overwhelming sense of pride. "We did it," he said, his voice full of emotion. "We're ready."

The group smiled, their bond stronger than ever. The Trial of the Guardians had pushed them to their limits, but it had also shown them just how powerful they were when they stood together.

As they made their way back through the forest, they knew that their journey was far from over. But they also knew that, no matter what challenges lay ahead, they were ready to face them—together.

Chapter 19: The Final Revelation

With the Trial of the Guardians behind them, Jayden and his friends felt more connected to the Quantum Path than ever before. They had faced their deepest fears and come out stronger, but there was still one lingering question—what was the true purpose of the Quantum Path, and how were they supposed to fulfill it?

The answer, they knew, lay with the mysterious figure who had been shadowing them since the beginning. The ancient manuscript they had found hinted at a final confrontation, a moment when the true nature of the Quantum Path would be revealed. But the specifics were vague, leaving the group uncertain about what to expect.

As they gathered in the park to discuss their next move, the device that had guided them all along activated once more. A new message appeared on the screen:

"The time for answers is upon you. Seek the Heart of the Path, where all will be revealed."

The group exchanged glances, a mix of excitement and apprehension in their eyes. The Heart of the Path—the name alone suggested that it was the key to everything they had been searching for.

"Any idea where this Heart of the Path might be?" Liam asked, looking around at the others.

Emily pulled out the manuscript, flipping through the pages for any clues. "There's a section here that mentions a place where the Quantum Path converges, where its energy is strongest. It's described as a hidden location, one that can only be found by those who are truly connected to the Path."

Kai nodded, his mind racing. "If the Path has been guiding us all along, maybe it'll lead us to this place too."

Jayden agreed. "We need to trust the Path. It's brought us this far, and I have a feeling it'll show us the way."

With renewed determination, the group set out once more, this time with no clear destination in mind. They let the device guide them, following its subtle signals and trusting in their connection to the Quantum Path. As they walked, the familiar landscape of their town began to change. The air grew heavier with energy, and the world around them seemed to shimmer with an otherworldly light.

After what felt like hours, they found themselves standing before a large, ancient tree, its roots twisting and winding into the ground like veins. The tree was unlike any they had seen before—its bark was a deep, shimmering silver, and its leaves glowed with a soft, ethereal light.

"This has to be it," Emily whispered, her voice filled with awe. "The Heart of the Path."

As they approached the tree, the device pulsed rapidly, confirming their suspicions. But before they could get any closer, a figure stepped out from behind the tree, blocking their path.

It was him—the mysterious figure who had been following them. He was dressed in dark, flowing robes, his face obscured by a hood. But there was no mistaking the aura of power that radiated from him.

"So, you've finally made it," the figure said, his voice cold and emotionless. "I wondered if you would."

Jayden stepped forward, his heart pounding. "Who are you? Why have you been trying to stop us?"

The figure chuckled, a low, sinister sound. "Stop you? No, I've been guiding you. Every step you've taken has led you here, to this moment. You were always meant to find the Heart of the Path. The only question is—what will you do with the power it holds?"

Liam frowned, suspicion in his eyes. "Power? What are you talking about?"

The figure's eyes glinted from beneath his hood. "The Quantum Path is more than just a journey of self-discovery. It's a source of unimaginable power, a force that can shape reality itself. Those who control the Path control the fate of the world."

The group stared at the figure, the weight of his words sinking in. The Quantum Path wasn't just a spiritual journey—it was a key to controlling the very fabric of existence.

Jayden's mind raced as he tried to process this revelation. "But the Path isn't about control.

It's about connection, about finding your true purpose."

The figure laughed again, a harsh, mocking sound. "That's what they want you to believe. But the truth is, the Path is a tool, a weapon that can be wielded by those with the will to do so.
And I intend to wield it."

Kai clenched his fists, anger boiling inside him. "You're wrong. The Path isn't something to be used for power. It's about something much deeper."

The figure's expression darkened. "You're naive, all of you. You've been given a gift, and you're too blind to see its true potential. But no matter—I've waited long enough. The power of the Quantum Path will be mine, whether you like it or not."

With a wave of his hand, the figure unleashed a burst of energy, sending the group flying backward. Jayden and his friends struggled to their feet, their bodies aching from the impact.

"We can't let him take the Path," Emily said, her voice filled with determination. "We have to stop him."

Jayden nodded, feeling a surge of resolve. "We've come this far. We can't let everything we've worked for be destroyed."

The group stood together, ready to face the figure. But before they could make a move, the tree behind them began to glow brighter, its light intensifying until it enveloped the entire clearing. The figure stepped back, shielding his eyes from the blinding light.

Suddenly, the light dimmed, revealing a vision—a vision of the Quantum Path, stretching out before them like a vast, glowing road. Figures walked along the Path, their forms flickering with energy. Some of the figures were familiar—they were the guardians who had come before Jayden and his friends, each of them carrying the legacy of the Path.

One of the figures, a woman with a calm, serene expression, stepped forward, her voice echoing in their minds. "The Quantum Path is not a weapon. It is a guide, a force that connects all living beings. Those who walk the Path do so not to gain power, but to fulfill a higher purpose— to protect and nurture the world around them."

The figure in the hood sneered. "Foolishness! Power is the only true purpose. And I will take it, no matter what you say."

The woman's gaze turned to Jayden and his friends. "The Path has chosen you, not to control it, but to protect it. The power you seek lies not in dominance, but in understanding, in connection. You must remember this as you face your final challenge."

The vision began to fade, leaving the group standing once more in the clearing. The figure in the hood, now visibly shaken, clenched his fists in anger. "I won't be denied. The Path will be mine!"

Jayden felt a surge of energy flowing through him, the words of the vision resonating deep within his soul. "No," he said firmly. "The Quantum Path isn't yours to take. It belongs to everyone, and we won't let you corrupt it."

The figure snarled, drawing upon the energy of the Path to launch another attack. But this time, Jayden and his friends were ready. Together, they channeled the power of the Quantum Path, their connection to each other strengthening their resolve.

The final battle was intense, a clash of wills and energies as the figure tried to seize control of the Path. But Jayden and his friends stood strong, their bond unbreakable. They fought not just for themselves, but for the future of the Path and the world it connected.

In the end, it was their unity that made the difference. The figure's power began to wane, his attacks growing weaker as he realized that he could not break the connection between the guardians. With one final, desperate attempt, the figure unleashed all the energy he had left, but it was not enough.

Jayden, Emily, Kai, and Liam stood together, their combined strength overwhelming the figure. With a final burst of energy, they repelled his attack, sending him crashing to the ground.

The figure lay there, defeated, his power drained. The clearing grew silent as the group caught their breath, the weight of what they had just accomplished sinking in.

Jayden stepped forward, his voice calm but firm. "It's over. The Quantum Path will remain as it was meant to be—a guide, not a weapon."

The figure glared at him, but there was no fight left in him. "You've won this time," he spat, his voice filled with bitterness. "But the struggle for power never ends."

With those final words, the figure dissolved into the air, leaving nothing behind but the faintest trace of dark energy.

The group stood there, the tension slowly dissipating as they realized they had truly won. The Heart of the Path glowed softly behind them, a symbol of the victory they had achieved—not just over the figure, but over the temptation to misuse the power they had been given.

As they left the clearing, Jayden felt a sense of peace settle over him. They had protected the Quantum Path, and in doing so, they had discovered its true purpose. The journey had changed them all, but it had also brought them closer together, forging a bond that would last a lifetime.

Chapter 20: The Legacy of the Quantum Path

The defeat of the mysterious figure marked the end of one journey for Jayden and his friends, but it was also the beginning of another. As they stood together in the clearing, the Heart of the Path continued to glow softly, a reminder of the power they had protected and the responsibility that came with it.

They had won the battle, but the true challenge was just beginning—how to use the knowledge they had gained to guide the world and ensure that the Quantum Path remained a force for good.

As they made their way back to the town, the energy of the Quantum Path seemed to follow them, surrounding them with a sense of calm and purpose. The experience had changed them, each in their own way, but it had also brought them closer together as a group. They knew that whatever lay ahead, they would face it together.

Back in town, life seemed to return to normal, but for Jayden and his friends, everything felt different. They were more aware of the world around them, more attuned to the subtle energies that connected all living things. The Quantum Path had opened their eyes to a deeper reality, one that few people ever glimpsed.

As they gathered at their usual spot in the park, the group reflected on everything they had been through. The trials, the battles, the revelations—they had all led to this moment, where they had a chance to make a real difference in the world.

"We've come so far," Emily said, her voice filled with emotion. "I can't believe how much we've changed since we first started this journey."

Kai nodded, a thoughtful expression on his face. "It's like we've been given a gift, something that goes beyond just power or knowledge.

We've been given the chance to shape the future, to make sure the Path is used for good."

Liam, ever the practical one, added, "But we have to be careful. The figure we fought might be gone, but there will always be others who seek to misuse the Path. We need to stay vigilant." Jayden agreed, but there was also a sense of hope in his heart. "We've learned so much, and we've grown stronger together. The Path chose us for a reason, and I believe we can protect it—and use it to help others."

The group sat in silence for a moment, each of them lost in their own thoughts. They knew that their journey was far from over, but they also knew that they were ready for whatever came next.

In the weeks that followed, Jayden and his friends began to explore new ways to use their connection to the Quantum Path. They realized that their role as guardians was not just to protect the Path, but to share its teachings with others, to help people understand the deeper connections that bound them together.

They started small, using their newfound knowledge to improve their own lives and the lives of those around them. Kai used his skills to create projects that promoted sustainability and harmony with nature, while Emily applied her strategic mind to help solve problems in their community. Liam, always the voice of reason, focused on bringing people together, fostering a sense of unity and cooperation.

Jayden, as the leader, found himself drawn to teaching. He began to share the lessons they had learned with others, helping them to see the world through the lens of the Quantum Path. He knew that not everyone would understand, but he also knew that even a small spark could ignite great change.

As they continued their work, the group began to notice subtle changes in the world around them. People seemed more connected, more aware of the impact of their actions. The energy of the Quantum Path, once hidden and mysterious, was now a guiding force, subtly influencing the world in positive ways.

One day, as they gathered in the park, the device that had guided them from the beginning activated once more. A final message appeared on the screen:

"The Path is eternal, but its guardians must evolve. You have fulfilled your role, but there will always be others who seek to follow in your footsteps. Guide them, teach them, and the Path will remain strong."

The message filled the group with a sense of closure, but also with a new sense of purpose. Their journey as guardians was not over—it was evolving. They had protected the Quantum Path, but now it was time to pass on what they had learned to the next generation.

Jayden looked at his friends, a smile on his face. "We've done something amazing, but it's just the beginning. The Path will continue, and so will we."

The group nodded, a shared understanding passing between them. They had been chosen to walk the Quantum Path, but their true legacy would be in how they guided others to do the same.

As they left the park, the sun setting behind them, they knew that the Quantum Path would always be a part of their lives. It had shaped them, challenged them, and ultimately brought them together. And in the end, that was the true power of the Path—the connections it created, the bonds it strengthened, and the hope it inspired.

Chapter 21: The Eternal Path

As the weeks turned into months, Jayden and his friends settled into their new roles as guardians and mentors. The Quantum Path, once a hidden mystery, had become a guiding light in their lives. They continued to explore its depths, discovering new ways to connect with its energy and share its teachings with others.

The changes in their town were subtle but profound. People seemed more in tune with one another, more aware of the impact of their actions on the world around them. The sense of unity that Jayden and his friends had worked so hard to foster was beginning to take root, spreading beyond their small circle and into the wider community.

But despite the positive changes, Jayden knew that their work was far from finished. The message from the device had made it clear that the Quantum Path was eternal, and that there would always be new challenges to face, new guardians to guide.

One evening, as the group gathered at the park, Jayden felt a sense of anticipation in the air. The sun was setting, casting a golden glow over the trees, and the energy of the Quantum Path seemed to hum with a quiet intensity.

"It feels different tonight," Kai said, breaking the silence. "Like something big is about to happen."

Emily nodded in agreement. "I've been feeling it too. I think we're about to receive our final task."

Liam, always the realist, added, "Whatever it is, we're ready for it. We've come this far, and we're not about to back down now."

As if on cue, the device activated once more, its screen glowing with a soft, warm light. A new message appeared, one that filled Jayden with a sense of both excitement and resolve:

"The Path continues, and so must you. Your final task is to pass on what you have learned, to ensure that the Path remains open for those who come after you. Seek out those who are ready to walk the Path, and guide them on their journey. This is your legacy."

The message was clear—Jayden and his friends were to become mentors, guiding the next generation of guardians along the Quantum Path. It was a daunting responsibility, but one that they were ready to embrace.

Jayden looked at his friends, seeing the determination in their eyes. "This is it. We've been given a new mission, and it's up to us to make sure the Path stays strong."

Kai smiled, a hint of excitement in his voice. "We're not just guardians anymore. We're teachers, leaders. This is our chance to make a real difference."

Emily, always the strategist, added, "We'll need to be careful, though. Not everyone will be ready for the Path, and we have to make sure that those we guide are truly prepared."

Liam nodded in agreement. "But we've learned so much, and we've grown stronger together. We can do this."

With the plan in place, the group began to search for those who might be ready to walk the Quantum Path. They started with the people they knew, friends and classmates who had shown signs of curiosity or connection to the Path's energy. They shared their knowledge carefully, always mindful of the responsibilities that came with the power they were offering.

As they mentored the new guardians, Jayden and his friends found that they were learning just as much as they were teaching. Each new connection deepened their understanding of the Quantum Path, revealing new layers of meaning and purpose. The Path was not just a journey, but a living, evolving force that grew stronger with each new person who walked it.

One day, as they were guiding a new group of guardians, Jayden felt a sudden surge of energy, stronger than anything he had experienced before. The air around him seemed to shimmer, and for a moment, he felt as if he could see the entire Quantum Path stretching out before him, its light connecting every living being in a vast, intricate web.

In that moment, Jayden understood the true nature of the Quantum Path. It was not just a road to be traveled, but a connection to the very essence of life itself. Every step they had taken, every challenge they had faced, had been part of a greater journey—one that would continue long after they were gone.

As the vision faded, Jayden felt a deep sense of peace. The Quantum Path was eternal, and so was the legacy they were creating. They had fulfilled their role as guardians, but their journey was far from over. There would always be new challenges, new guardians to guide, and new paths to explore.

And with that realization, Jayden knew that he and his friends were ready for whatever the future held. They had become more than just travelers on the Quantum Path—they had become its keepers, its protectors, and its teachers.

Together, they would continue to walk the Path, passing on its wisdom to those who were ready to follow. The Quantum Path would remain strong, its light guiding those who sought it, just as it had guided them.

As the sun set on that final day, Jayden and his friends stood together, looking out at the world they had helped to shape. The future was uncertain, but they knew that they were ready for whatever came next.

The Quantum Path was eternal, and so was the legacy they would leave behind.

* 9 7 9 8 8 9 5 8 8 8 7 0 4 *